Strictly for Laughs

Ellen Conford

Strictly for Laughs

Pacer Books
a member of The Putnam Publishing Group
New York

Pacer Books are published by
The Putnam Young Readers Group
51 Madison Avenue
New York, New York 10010

Book design by Ellen S. Levine
Printed in the United States of America
First Printing

Library of Congress Cataloging in Publication Data
Conford, Ellen.
Strictly for laughs.
Summary: an aspiring disc jockey and an aspiring
comedian find their comfortable relationship
becomes quite stormy when they get their big chance
to pursue their dreams.
[1. Comedians—Fiction.   2. Radio broadcasting—
Fiction] I. Title.
PZ7.C7593St.   1985   [Fic]   85-9450
ISBN 0-448-47754-8

To David, on our twenty-fifth anniversary:
You changed my flat tire in the rain,
October 23, 1959, and have been sending me
into transports of delight ever since.

Strictly for Laughs

One

"Your own show? On the radio?" I rolled my eyes up until only the whites showed. "I'm dying."

It was a bleak January Monday. We were sitting in Peter's car in the McDonald's parking lot. We always avoid the school cafeteria on Mondays. That's when they serve fish sticks.

"It's for three Saturday nights," Peter said. "From midnight to two. I just hope somebody listens."

"Anybody who gets home from a date between midnight and two will listen," I said. "Assuming they listen to WRTP at all."

"They listen to Dakota Stone," he said. "Once they find out she isn't on, they might turn me off."

Dakota Stone was WRTP's weekend woman. She came on with a husky, suggestive voice, like she was trying to seduce you into listening to the records. She certainly never seduced me. Her records were the

9

schmaltzy "adult contemporary sound" that WRTP played every night.

"Dakota Stone," I scoffed. "Music for late-night lovers." I made my voice low and sexy. "Come real close to your radio and let's listen to this one together...." I did a pretty fair imitation of Dakota's breathy delivery. Actually I can do a pretty fair imitation of almost anyone. My Donald Duck is legendary.

"She doesn't do a thing for me," I said.

"I don't think she's supposed to do anything for you, Joey. I think she's supposed to do something for *me.*"

"And does she do anything for you?" I leered at him over my Big Mac.

"She's thirty years older than me and has two kids."

"That doesn't answer my question."

Peter smiled slyly.

Which still didn't answer my question. As far as I knew, Peter was immune to the potent lure of sensual women. Including me. I figured he was just a slow developer and there was nothing I could do to speed him up. But if he was finally developing, maybe I should cut down the wisecracks and turn on the sweet talk.

It wouldn't be easy doing a complete one-eighty after all these years. Besides, I had my image to maintain.

I nibbled thoughtfully on a french fry.

Back in the sixth grade I wrote a comedy skit and performed it with my friend April Abruzzo. She didn't mind playing straight woman. We brought down the house, as they say in show biz, and won first prize.

I always was the class cutup. Some teachers called me other names, but that prize and the kids laughing and cheering told me more than any aptitude test I could ever take.

I was a million laughs, and the world was going to laugh with me.

But I'd do it on my own. Solo. Even at twelve, April drove male audiences to distraction, and I didn't want half of my audience distracted while I was on. I needed to know that the applause was all for me.

I met Peter two years later. He was such a nice, quiet boy. A little shy and withdrawn, but he seemed so mature. He had sandy hair, clear intelligent blue eyes, and he walked erect—which set him apart from most of the nerds in eighth grade.

By this time I was convinced that my wit was irresistible. I was also convinced that Peter needed me. He was an introvert and I was just the person to bring him out of his shell.

I did coax him out, at least a little bit further than your average sleeping turtle, and he seemed to appreciate the attention.

As I got to know him better, I learned that he appeared mature mostly because he kept his feelings to himself and didn't guffaw when some guy showed him a copy of *Playboy* disguised as a math workbook.

As Peter got to know me better, he learned that I was a yock a minute. Even though he hid his feelings, I could sometimes sense when he was down and tease him out of it.

The way I saw it, my aim in life was to make people laugh. So that's what I did. I mean, what's more depressing than a depressed comedian? As far as Peter or anyone else knew, nothing fazed good old Joey Merino.

But then we started high school. And suddenly I realized that I was deeply, passionately, hopelessly in love with Peter. Unfortunately, Peter was deeply, passionately, obsessively in love with his uncle's radio station.

I began to hang out with him whenever I took a break from working on my comedy routines, and he hung out at WRTP every chance he got.

This was nothing new. He'd always dreamed of being a deejay, and RTP had been his second home since he was seven, but now his single-mindedness frustrated me. I wondered if he knew there were opposite sexes, and if he ever noticed that I was a member of the opposition.

I took to dropping a few subtle hints, like asking him if he thought show business marriages could be successful, and humming "I'm in the Mood for Love" whenever there was a lull in our conversation. I even asked him to take me to the freshman dance. But our relationship remained as comfortable as an old flannel shirt, and just about as romantic.

I tried out all my comic monologues on him, and he talked about radio.

What else could I do? If I hit him with "I love you," he'd probably panic and spend the rest of high school hiding in his locker. I didn't want to ruin a beautiful friendship, especially since it had become the only close friendship I had.

Now, as I licked ketchup off my fingers, I wondered

if Peter had finally discovered that he wanted more than just a good buddy.

"... and Uncle Charlie said I can intern at the station next year," he was saying. "Isn't that great?"

"Not exactly the shock of the year," I remarked.

Peter had been hoping to train at RTP. We both planned to go to the same local college my brother Matt attended. I could take performance courses while I tried out for some showcase clubs.

Peter's uncle hadn't given him a definite answer about the interning up till now, but knowing Uncle Charlie, the suspense was extremely bearable.

"Well, it's nice to know for sure," he said.

"Listen, Peter, when you fill in for Dakota Stone, do me a favor? Play some decent music. Every time I have insomnia I switch on your station. Five minutes and I'm off to Lullabyeland. No joke."

I took a hearty bite of my Big Mac. RTP is an all-talk station during the day, but at night they switch to that "adult contemporary" sound. I've heard more exciting music in the dentist's office.

"Forget about decent music," Peter said. "They don't own any. But Uncle Charlie said I could do anything I wanted. I don't just have to play music."

I put my Big Mac on the dashboard of the car. I carefully wiped the Special Sauce off my chin with my napkin. I grabbed Peter's arm.

"Anything you want?" I said. "You've got two hours on the radio to do anything you want?"

"Right. And to tell you the truth, I'm a little—"

13

"Anything at all?"

"Right. But I'm not sure what—"

"Like, for instance, having guest stars?"

"I never thought about bringing anyone else on the show," Peter said doubtfully. "I mean, it's my show. My uncle said—"

"That you could do anything you wanted." I felt a little shiver as my pulse speeded up—and it had nothing to do with sitting so close to Peter. I could see it all so clearly! As clearly as I saw it the night of the sixth grade talent show. This was it—my big break. I would do a routine on Peter's show, someone would hear me. Some bigshot. There would be a phone call. "Miss Merino? I caught you on that radio show—you know, Peter What'shisname?—and I wonder if you'd be interested in—"

"I'm ready!" I cried. "I am *ready!*"

"Ready for what?"

I dug my fingers right through Peter's jacket till I could feel bone under the flesh under the wool.

"Ow!"

"We're a team, Peter. We go together like ham and eggs, Mutt and Jeff, Spic 'n' Span . . . Romeo and Juliet."

"Since when have we been a team?" He pried my fingers off his arm.

"Oh, Peter, since forever. Since eighth grade. Since you sent me that valentine 'To a good friend across the miles.' Since I taught you the box step for the freshman dance. Since you got your own radio show."

"My mother taught me the box step," he said irrit-

14

ably. "And we were the only people in that whole gym doing the box step to 'Chainsaw Lover.'"

"Now don't get Oedipal. The point is, we've been friends for a long time. And we can be completely honest with each other, can't we?"

"Within reason," he muttered.

"You're a terrific person, Peter, you really are, and you have a lot of fine qualities—"

"*But?*"

"But let's face it. You're not the most extroverted person in the world. That's why you *need* me. What happens if you get in front of that microphone and freeze up?"

I knew my motives were not entirely altruistic. I wanted to get in front of that microphone as much as Peter did. But after all, he'd never been on the radio in his life. He once told me, sort of embarrassed, that he used to practice his deejay voice all the time with a tape recorder when he was in junior high, but only when his mother wasn't home.

That's a lot different than broadcasting live from a real studio, where fifty thousand people might be listening to you.

Fifty thousand people! Think of the exposure! Think of the opportunities! Think of Johnny Carson accidentally tuning in.

"With me there you'll be more relaxed," I persisted. "It'll take a lot of the pressure off. If you get mike fright I'll be right by your side to rescue you. Just think of the emotional support I can give you."

15

Just think of the air time I'll get if Peter panics. Not nice, Joey, I told myself. *Not nice.* You don't wish for a friend to fail so you can succeed. I didn't really mean it.

"You're doing a great job of building my confidence right now," he said. "Lunch period's almost over. We'd better get back."

"Peter, please. Please let me be on your show. Just once, just for a few minutes. Peter, I want to be a star!"

"All my life," he began, "I wanted to be a deejay. Since I was four years old and my uncle took me to WRTP for the first time...."

I nearly tuned him out. I'd heard this a million times. He'd begun to sound like Ted Baxter on the Mary Tyler Moore reruns. "It all started in a little five-thousand-watt station in Fresno, California...."

"I don't want a partner, Joey. Don't you understand? I didn't think I'd get to go on the air for another year— and my own show. It's unbelievable. We may be a team for everything else, but not for this. This is *mine.*"

I tossed my almost untouched Big Mac into the bag. Actually, I did understand. Who better? I'm not good at sharing the spotlight either.

"You didn't eat much." He collected the boxes and the napkins to throw in the trash can.

"I don't feel hungry." All I felt was dejected. Like he'd dangled a diamond ring in front of me and then snatched it away.

"Listen, Peter, you want to be a solo act, and so do I. But all I'm asking for is one chance. You have two other shows to do all by yourself, and next year prob-

16

ably a lot more. I only want a few minutes. Just once. Your uncle's doing it for you, and you're the only one who can do it for me. No joke."

I looked at him, pleading with my eyes. No funny patter now, all kidding aside. This was from my heart. I don't think Peter had ever seen me this serious or this unhappy in his life.

Maybe that got to him. Suddenly he got a glimpse of a vulnerable side that he never knew I had. Maybe I didn't know it myself. He always believed he needed me more than I needed him. I guess I let him believe that.

He shifted his gaze, like he didn't want to see what was in my eyes.

"I'll think about it," he said finally.

"Oh, Peter!" I could have shot straight up through the roof of his Lynx. "Oh, Peter, I love you madly!" I threw myself on his shoulder and pretended to faint.

"Good old Joey," he said dryly. "Remember, I only promised to think about it."

I paced the floor in front of my brother Matt's room, waiting for him to get off the phone. This could take months. He was talking to his girlfriend, Monique. Monique—can you believe it? She even looked like a Monique. She was tall and slim and blond and always seemed to be posing for a Swedish travel poster.

Matt and my fifteen-year-old brother Andy and I all have phones in our rooms, but they're on the same line. We've campaigned for private lines, but my parents say that four numbers for a family of five is obscene, and the phone company will charge us business rates.

So we share the same number, which is listed in the directory as "Children's Phone." We think that's demeaning, and we're not very good at sharing. Three teenagers scrambling to use one telephone gives new meaning to the term sibling rivalry.

It was ten o'clock and I had to call Peter. He'd had plenty of time to "think about it" by now. I couldn't wait another second to find out his decision.

Finally I pounded on Matt's door. "Your ninety minutes are up! *I need that phone!*" I threw the door open and charged into his room.

Matt smiled and lazily swung his feet down from the bed, where he'd propped them in his favorite back-on-the-floor, legs raised, telephone posture. "Got to sign off now, Monique. Little Chubby Cheeks is throwing a tantrum."

Chubby Cheeks? I bared my teeth. I had to throw something, so I grabbed the first thing I laid my hands on and hurled it at his head.

Unfortunately it was only a pair of sweat socks.

He hung up and I stormed out of the room, slamming the door after me. I was just about to dial Peter's number when I glanced casually at the mirror.

"Matt?" I yelled. "I don't really have chubby cheeks, do I?"

"Only when you smile," he yelled back.

I smile a *lot*. I smiled into the mirror. *God.* My cheeks nearly puffed up over my eyelids. Maybe I ought to suck my face in and try to look gaunt.

What am I *doing?* Who cares about my cheeks? Anyway, Carol Burnett has chubby cheeks. So does Gilda Radner. Lily Tomlin doesn't, but—*stop with the stupid cheeks already!* The important thing is, will Peter let you be on his show?

I sucked my cheeks in and dialed Peter's number.

"Peter? Did you know I can make coffee?"

"I'll bet you can count to ten, too."

"I'm going to ignore that," I said, "because as long as you hold the key to my entire future happiness, I want to stay on your good side and be helpful and ingratiating. I make very good coffee."

"That's nice," he said. "Why are you telling me this?"

"You're doing a midnight-to-two A.M. show. You'll need coffee to stay awake. I'm willing to come there and make you fresh coffee—not instant, you understand. I'll even serve it to you in a nice, big mug, none of those cruddy Styrofoam cups—"

"Joey, I don't drink coffee."

"Tea. Cocoa. Fresh squeezed orange juice. *Zombies,*" I said desperately. "Limeade. I will personally crush the limes with my bare feet. Peter, I'm groveling. I'll do anything to get on your show. Listen to me—I'm crawling. How does it feel to know I'm down on my hands and knees, debasing myself like this just for a few minutes of your precious air time?"

"Not bad," he replied.

"You brute!" I shouted. "One taste of power and you turn into a heartless tyrant. Why are you doing this to me? I bared my soul to you—"

"Joey."

"Attila the Hun," I raged. "This is a whole new side of you, Peter, and I don't think I—"

"Joey."

"—know a person for years and think you're friends—"

"Joey! Will you shut up a minute. You can be on the show."

"You mean it?" I leaped off the bed and clutched the phone to my ear with both hands to make sure I was hearing right.

"I can't believe it! We're going to be so great! What a team! Stillman and Merino. Notice how I put your name first?"

"Hey, I never said—"

"Listen, Peter, about my opening monologue—"

"This is *my* show—"

"Oh, Peter, you don't know how happy you've made me. You don't know what this means to me. Well, of course you do, but—" I was babbling. "You know what? Tomorrow I'm going to give you a great, big sloppy kiss that's going to knock your socks off."

"I'd rather see you crawl!"

Two

By Tuesday afternoon, at least sixteen people had come up to me to ask if it was true that Peter and I were going to have our own radio show. I don't know how word spread so fast. I only mentioned it to a couple of people.

Of course, after I'd spoken to Peter last night, I dashed out of my room, stood at the top of the stairs and screamed, "I'm going to be on the radio! I'm going to be a *star!*"

I guess Andy must have gotten the news out. He's only a sophomore, but he's got a lot of friends at James P. Jefferson.

As I waited for Peter on the front steps of the school I was so elated I could hardly stand still. Most of the kids I'd talked to had reacted with surprise that Peter was going to be on the radio at all. "You should have your own program," they said. "What's *he* going to do?"

"Well, after all," I replied modestly, "it *is* his uncle's station."

I got so dizzy with all the attention that I began to feel like I was already a star. Brimming with enthusiasm and confidence, I greeted Peter with a giggle. "You want your socks knocked off now, Big Boy, or should I wait till we're alone?"

"You want your block knocked off now, or should *I* wait till we're alone?" Peter snarled.

"You don't seem to be in a very good mood," I observed. "What's the matter?"

"Where do you get off telling people *we're* going to be on the radio?"

"But we are, aren't we?"

"This is *my* show, not *our* show. You better get that straight right from the start or your career is over before it begins."

"Yes, master. Yes, master." I bowed my head in submission.

"I'm not kidding, Joey," he said. "Don't joke about this."

"But that's what you pay me for."

He stuffed his hands in his pockets and stomped down the steps. He was walking so fast I had to jog to keep up with him. My books bounced up and down in my arms.

"Maybe I did get a little carried away," I admitted, "but really, it must have been Andy who got the facts mixed up. I know it's your show. I'll straighten it out tomorrow, I promise. I mean, anybody who got the wrong impression—Peter, don't be mad at me. I don't

22

blame you if you are, but..." I was breathless from trying to keep up with him and apologize at the same time. "You want me to grovel some more?"

He slowed down. He even smiled a little. "I guess that's enough groveling."

"Good. It's really not my style at all." I'd never seen Peter so angry before—at least, not at me.

"You nearly blew that kiss I promised you," I said lightly.

He stopped walking. I stopped too. Why had I brought that up again? All at once I felt embarrassed. He looked at me strangely, like he was trying to figure out whether this was just another joke or if I really wanted to kiss him.

I was trying to figure out the same thing. I mean, naturally I wanted to kiss him—though I'd rather *he* wanted to kiss *me*—but for a moment there seemed to be a sort of self-consciousness between us that had never been there before.

I didn't know what to say to get us back to normal again. So I fell back on my usual method of dealing with an uncomfortable situation.

I parted my lips in a sexy pout, breathed heavily, and crossed my eyes.

He laughed. "Good old Joey," he said. "Always the kidder."

"I made some notes last night," Peter said. We sat at his kitchen table with two Cokes and a bunch of looseleaf paper.

"This doesn't seem very professional," I commented.

"Shouldn't we have one of those big charts and some Magic Markers?"

We were alone in his house. His mother works in a real estate office and his father hasn't been home since Peter was three years old. He just walked out on them, and they hadn't heard from him in fifteen years. You don't have to be much of a psychologist to figure that being abandoned by a father is bound to have an effect on a kid, even though Peter's Uncle Charlie had done everything he could to be a surrogate. I don't know if anyone ever gets over a thing like that.

"We can struggle along without the Magic Markers," Peter said. "What I really need are ideas."

"For starters," I suggested, "I can do my opening monologue."

"No. No opening monologue."

"What do you mean? That's the reason I was supposed to—"

"Not for you. It's my show, and if anyone does an opening monologue, it should be me."

"Well, sure," I agreed. "Naturally. I meant the monologue I do after you do yours."

"You're not going to do any monologues. What I thought was, I'd start by introducing myself, then play a few records to get rolling. You know, sort of get the feel of the mike. Then we'll bring up some hot, controversial topic and take phone calls."

"What do you mean, 'we'?" I asked, outraged. "You've got this all planned already. The whole point of my being on the show was to do my routines. Now you're

24

saying I can't do any? What is this? Am I really only going to make coffee?"

"Joey, you're not listening. 'We' means 'we.' As in 'you and I.' A team, remember? Ham and eggs, Spic 'n' Span?"

I noticed he didn't mention Romeo and Juliet, but I didn't care. I had no idea what was going on, what he was talking about.

"You just finished telling me this was *your* show. Since when are we a team again?"

"Since you got me thinking about freezing up in front of the microphone." He looked down at his looseleaf pages, avoiding my eyes. "I'm—uh—a little nervous. I started thinking, maybe it would be a good idea to have someone around. Two hours is a long time."

I was so confused that I felt like I needed an interpreter. "You keep saying, 'It's *my* show, not our show,' yesterday you said you were going to play records and be a regular deejay, like you always wanted, today you want me on the show but you don't want me to do anything, at least not anything I want to do." I shook my head as if I could clear it. "What *are* you saying?"

"I'm saying, maybe you were right." His voice was low, but he finally looked me in the eye. "Maybe I do need you for the first show. Maybe just for moral support. Maybe having you there—like you said, I'm not the most extroverted person in the world."

"Listen, Peter. I never meant to make you feel like you couldn't do it," I said. Though I couldn't help thinking about all those kids who thought I was the

25

one who should have my own show. "All I wanted was a little exposure. What do I know about radio? I mean, you've been practicing for this all your life."

"You didn't make me feel like I couldn't do it," he said. "Ever since my uncle sprung this on me I've been nervous. Listen," he said earnestly, "you give me confidence. You always do. You're always there when I need you." He put his hand on my arm.

I wanted to reach out to him and put my arms around him and hug him. I held back, waiting to see what he would do.

"Joey, I'm so tense," he said. He took his hand off my arm.

I don't think he heard me sigh. I was used to feeling responsible for bringing Peter out of himself, for being his best friend. I knew he needed me, even though I wanted him to love me, not just need me. But maybe this was the first step—opening up enough to tell me he was scared.

I remembered yesterday, when it seemed that the balance of our relationship had tilted because he was the one who could give me my first opportunity at stardom. I remembered how I called him Attila the Hun, how I accused him of reveling in his sudden power over me.

Now *I* seemed to be holding the reins again. I wasn't sure I wanted them. No matter what Peter said, part of his panic was my fault. I didn't like being responsible for that.

"You're going to be fine," I said firmly. "I know you are. But if you want me to be there, I'll be there. Now,

26

would you please tell me what it is I'm going to *do* once I *get* there?"

Peter's face brightened. "Good old Joey. I can always count on you."

Ohh, Peter, of course you can count on me. Start with my fingers and work your way up my arm to my lips. You can count the number of kisses it takes to get from my arm to my lips. You can run your fingers through my hair. Or I could run my fingers through your hair. Anything you want.

"The first thing is, we have to think up topics for the phone-in segment. Every topic I came up with sounded boring."

Compared to my steamy scenario, dredging up controversy sounded positively yawn-making. But I was used to keeping my lips on hold and repressing the urge to fling myself at Peter and cry, "You blind fool, can't you see what I'm trying to tell you? I *love* you!"

"How about the hidden Marxist symbolism in *The Attack of the Killer Tomatoes?*" I suggested glumly. "You know how they leave all those red stains."

"Too intellectual." He grinned. "Who do you think listens to RTP?"

"Two Cub Scouts, three expectant mothers, and all the patients in the county home for the incurably silly. No offense."

WRTP broadcasts on about twelve kilowatts and only reaches a limited area of central Long Island. They have a potential fifty thousand listeners, but at any given time I bet their audience could fit into a broom closet.

Two hours and three Cokes later, we'd programmed

the whole show in half-hour blocks. We'd thought up three fairly provocative issues for the phone-in segment. We could have had four, but Peter was unreasonably hostile to my idea that we discuss: "Should we change the entire format of this dumb station?"

But he loved my inspiration to play the oldest, corniest records we could find to kid RTP's nighttime "adult" music. We had a whole log for the show, all spelled out in Bic and white on Peter's notebook paper.

He was so cheered up now he looked like he could hardly sit still. He jumped up and did a few jogs around the kitchen. I stretched and yawned and discovered little kinks in various parts of my anatomy from sitting on a kitchen chair too long.

I was almost as up as he was. He'd finally agreed to let me do a monologue on the program.

"It's just that I didn't want to sound like Amateur Night," he explained.

And all the extra exposure I'd get—Peter planned that we would both talk to callers, and I imagined the chances I'd have to use my rapier wit bantering with the listeners. People would think, "What a brilliant comedic flair she has! Who is this incredible talent?"

Even though WRTP has such a limited audience, Dakota Stone's show always gets the highest ratings for the station, except for "Ask Dr. Waxman," their dial-a-shrink program. They also have a show called "Tooth or Consequences," where you can call up and ask dental questions, but it's not nearly as popular.

"I'd better get dinner started," Peter said. "My mother will be home any minute." He sprinted to the refrigerator. He looked so high he could have been bouncing on a trampoline. It was great to see him like this, to know that I'd helped give him some self-confidence.

He took a package of lamb chops out of the refrigerator. Peter is very competent in the kitchen. I could sit and watch him cook for hours. He's adorable when he cooks. So intense.

"So," he said, tossing the package of lamb chops on the counter, "when do I get my socks knocked off?"

I was stunned. Did I hear him right? Did he ask me to *take* his socks off or to *knock* them off with that big, sloppy kiss I'd promised him?

What do I do now?

My mind raced through the options. Do I make a big joke out of it? Is he serious? Is *he* making a joke out of it? Why did he say it? I thought we'd laughed the whole idea away a couple of hours ago.

Actually, my mind didn't race through any of these possibilities. It moved sluggishly, like when you walk in a dream and your legs feel like they're made of oatmeal.

But this was no dream. Here was the invitation I'd been waiting for, the chance to leap at Peter's lean, golden body and into his heart.

He stood by the sink, eyeing me. I got the distinct impression that he was beginning to have another anxiety attack. At this very moment, while I dithered over what to do, he might be regretting he'd issued the invitation. Any second now he might say, "But seriously, folks. . . ."

Before he had time to take it back, I batted my eyelashes and murmured, "Whatever you say, Big Boy."

I sucked in my cheeks so they wouldn't look chubby and slowly got up from the chair. I guess I must have walked toward him (or run toward him, I don't remember how I got there), and the next thing I knew, I had him bent backwards over the sink and was kissing him enthusiastically on the lips.

I think he whimpered or grunted or something. It was possible that I was breaking his back, bending him over the sink that way, but once I started kissing him I didn't want to stop.

I couldn't stop. I'd been saving up this kiss for three years, and no trivial qualms about permanent injury to Peter's spine were going to cool my fevered lips.

I don't remember whether he actually kissed me back or not. I seemed to be making all the smacking noises. He did have his arms around me, but he might not have been hugging me, only clutching me, for fear that if he didn't hold on I'd push him down the drain and he'd be ground up in the garbage disposal.

Suddenly I heard a voice behind me saying, "Oops."

Mrs. Stillman's voice.

Dizzily, I let go of Peter, but I had to grab the edge of the counter to keep the kitchen from spinning around.

Peter's mother cleared her throat. I tried to clear my head. Peter gasped for breath.

"Oh, Peter," Mrs. Stillman clucked, "lamb chops again?"

Three

I wouldn't say I spent a sleepless night, but your average goldfish closes his eyes more than I did. I wondered what had come over me. I wondered if Peter wondered what had come over me. I wondered if Peter's mother wondered why I had apparently tried to push her only son's head down the garbage disposal.

What should I do tomorrow when I see Peter? Should I explain? How could I explain? I didn't understand much of it myself. What I did understand, I didn't want to explain.

I remembered a quote from some famous rich woman: "Never apologize, never explain."

Sure, when you're mature and rich you can get away with that kind of an attitude, but when you're seventeen and a half and hurl yourself at someone who never suspected the depths of passion in your soul, some words of clarification might be in order.

What words? "Gee, I don't know what came over me?" "You made me do it. You said I promised?" "You blind fool, can't you see what I've been trying to tell you?" Or (innocently) "What kiss?"

The best thing might be to rely on the familiar: "When Joey Merino kisses 'em, they stay kissed." Or, "Did I knock your socks off or just melt your shoe-laces?" Or, "Want to see what I do for an encore?"

Somehow I didn't think any of these witticisms would reassure Peter that my loss of cool was a temporary aberration and we could go right back to being "just good friends," as if my torrid embrace had never happened.

But I don't *want* to be just good friends, I told myself.

Why should I try to calm him down when what I really wanted to do was steam him up? Why should he be calm? I thought. I'm not calm. I'm lying here not sleeping, obsessed with the thought of how it felt to kiss Peter.

I wondered if Peter was lying in his bed, not sleeping, spending his own restless night obsessed with me. Was he tossing and turning, trying to figure out my shocking lapse into lust? Or was he replaying my passion in his mind, deciding he liked my burning kisses and my cavewoman aggressiveness? Was he maybe even hoping to see what I *would* do for an encore?

Or was he tossing and turning because I'd rattled him, so that now he thought I was too rash and un-predictable to be allowed on the air? Once we were alone in the studio, there was no telling what I might say to shock the two Cub Scouts, the three expectant mothers, and all those incurably silly people out there in Radioland.

Wednesday morning I looked positively haggard. Hollywood makeup men work hours trying to transform young actresses into the sunken-eyed vampire that looked back at me from my mirror.

I'm not model-thin—in fact, I could lose five pounds and still not be thin—but today my face looked long and drawn, and my chubby cheeks sank in without any effort to make them look hollow.

It was amazing that not one person in my family noticed that I resembled a character from *Night of the Living Dead.* My mother commented that I looked a little tired, but nobody ran screaming from the table. Not even Andy, who will sometimes do that when I look perfectly charming. Maybe I didn't look as decomposed as I thought.

I got through breakfast without falling face first into my Raisin Bran. Peter honked his familiar honk at the regular time. I pulled on my coat and collected my books.

I prepared to face Peter.

My lightning wit, I reminded myself. My snappy patter, my quick comebacks. I'll think of something to say. Besides, I might not have to say a word. Peter might have realized, after a night of fevered dreams and soul-searching self-analysis, that he'd unconsciously been waiting for me to knock his socks off since ninth grade.

"What a blind fool I've been!" he'd cry, smacking himself in the forehead. "*Now* I see what you've been trying to tell me. Come here, Sugar Lips, and hold on to your socks."

"Hi, Joey. Sure is cold, isn't it?" Peter gunned the engine a few times as I settled into the front seat.

So much for facing Peter. Peter wasn't going to face anything. We weren't going to talk about it. We're going to pretend it never happened. We'll be "just good friends" again. For a change. Forever.

"Sure is cold," I said in my hillbilly voice. "You could freeze an egg on the sidewalk."

Peter chuckled, even though my snappy patter was a little soggy. I strapped myself into the seat belt. This is a pain in the neck, because in my bulky winter coat I feel like I'm in a straitjacket. But Peter won't start the car if you don't buckle your seat belt.

"Listen, are you doing anything this afternoon?" he asked as we rode down the street. "Because Uncle Charlie thought it would be a good idea for me to go over to RTP for sort of an orientation."

"Are you kidding? You've been hanging around that place for eleven years. What's left for you to orient?"

"I have to be sure I know how to work the equipment. I think I know all I have to already, just from watching, but don't you think I could use a little hands-on practice before Saturday night?"

What a straight line. I had to clamp my lips together to keep from telling him he needed a *lot* of hands-on practice.

"Good idea." I congratulated myself for not bursting into sarcastic laughter.

"I certainly could use some orientation," I said,

"considering that I'm going to be a co-host and I don't know a thing about radio."

"I didn't exactly say you were going to be my co-host, Joey," he mumbled.

"What?" I twisted around in the seat to look at him.

Peter is a very cautious driver. He adheres to the fifty-five-mile-per-hour speed limit, always slows down in a school zone, and he doesn't take his eyes off the road for an instant.

"Don't tell me," I said. "I'm back to making coffee, right?"

I *knew* it, I *knew* it. He thought I'd gone mental and was afraid that if he let me on the show I'd suddenly grab the mike and start spouting Homer's *Odyssey* in Pig Latin.

Just because of a little kiss? Did a person have to be certifiably whacko because she kissed another person? Or did Peter think I had to be certifiably whacko to want to kiss *him?*

Who cared about Peter's twisted psychology now? Who cared about Peter now? I mean, as a love object. He was welching on his promise. He was taking back my big break. He was shooting down my star. He was a ruthless monster.

I wish I *had* pushed him down the garbage disposal.

"I mean, I just don't want to call you my co-host," he explained. "I'm the show, remember?"

"And what am I? Ms. Coffee?"

He chuckled. If he didn't stop chuckling I'd strangle him with his seat belt. Which he always buckled up for safety.

"You're my guest star. My *special* guest star."

"And everything else is still the same?" I asked. "We're doing the program the way we planned it?"

"Sure. I told you, it's just that I don't want it to be the Peter and Joey Show."

"I get the picture." Boy, did I get the picture. He didn't want any part of "Stillman and Merino," professionally or romantically.

Okay. Fine. I can take a hint. As long as I get to do my bit on the radio and launch myself into the galaxy of young comic stars, I'll be satisfied.

Or so I told myself.

As the day wore on, I had to admit that I wasn't satisfied. It wasn't okay for Peter to pretend that our lips had never touched.

He rejected me, I reminded myself. He made it perfectly clear that he has no interest in touching lips with me. What's fine about that?

I kept trying to shake off my depression. After all, nothing was new or different; we'd always been platonic friends and that was that. I'd managed to control my feelings. Up until yesterday.

I told myself that the important thing was to wow the audience Saturday night, to make an impression— to create a demand for Joey Merino. This was a one-shot deal; if I didn't sell myself now, there was no telling when I'd get another break.

That afternoon we drove to WRTP for Peter's orientation. Fred Harris, the station manager, led us into

Studio B. It was a small, bright room, with a glass wall on one side separating the studio from the engineer's booth. There was a console facing the glass wall, a bank of microphones, and dials and switches and buttons. For all I knew it could have been the dashboard of a spaceship.

I was bewildered by all this high-tech equipment, but Peter had been sitting in RTP studios watching broadcasters work since he was seven. I'd only been here a couple of times.

Peter sat down at the console and touched a microphone timidly, as if it might explode. He shot me a look of panic. His eyes darted wildly from switch to switch, like he didn't know what any of this stuff was, as if he'd completely forgotten everything he'd ever learned.

"Dave Dayton will be in soon, but I just want to show you a few things first," Fred said. Dave Dayton does the afternoon drive-time show.

"Good. Fine. Thanks, Fred." Peter wiped his hands on his jeans. Poor Peter. He really must have a serious case of mike fright. He couldn't pull off his "everything's fine" act.

Fred pointed at something. "This is the kill switch."

"Nuclear or conventional?" I asked.

Fred eyed me suspiciously.

"Just a little joke," I said, "to break the tension."

"Not now, Joey," Peter said.

"Anything you don't want to go over the air, you push that button. It cuts off all transmission from in here. So if you take phone calls and somebody starts

37

screaming obscenities, you can cut him right off. You'll be on a seven-second delay, so there's going to be dead air every time you use the kill. Try not to hit it too often or you'll have a lot of gaps."

"What about people in the studio?" I asked. "Can he use that button to shut me up too?"

"There isn't a button in the world that could shut you up," Peter said. "Will you please shut up?"

"Yes, master." I bowed my head humbly.

Fred scowled. "She going to be on the show?"

What was the matter with him? All I'd done was make a little joke and he looked at me like I was something that scuttled across his kitchen floor at night.

"And why not?" I demanded. "I'm a million laughs. Ask anybody. Ask Peter. Peter, aren't I a million laughs?"

"Not right now you're not," he said tightly.

"What did I do? Was it something I said?"

Fred glared at me. Then he glared at Peter.

"Joey," Peter said, "there are times when being funny isn't funny. Will you please behave?"

"*Behave?* What am I, a child? A poodle? You want me to go stand in the corner?"

"Yes, dammit! Go stand in the corner!"

"Does your uncle know she's going to be on the show?" Fred Harris demanded.

What was going on here? All of a sudden everyone was picking on me.

"Joey, for once would you take me seriously?" Peter sighed. "I go on the air in forty-eight hours—"

"*We* go on the air," I reminded him.

"That's debatable!" he yelled. "I'm nervous enough, and I've got all this stuff to learn and you're messing around."

"You should get so lucky!" I snapped.

"I already did, remember?"

I could have kicked myself for popping off that way, and I was rattled to hear Peter blurt out anything about what we were going to pretend never happened.

Fred's eyes got all beady and his face puckered up like he'd just swigged a bottle of vinegar. He crammed some pills into his mouth.

"I'm sorry," I said meekly. "I'm here to learn too." What humility. I *was* sorry, but I sounded so humble I nearly made myself throw up.

Peter finally pulled himself together. "It'll be okay, Fred," he said in his normal voice. "Don't worry."

"Your uncle better make sure she learns her libel and slander laws," Fred warned.

"I'll memorize them," I promised.

The door to the studio opened. A middle-aged man came in lugging a bundle of papers, clipboards, magazines, and books.

"Hi, Pete," he said cheerfully. "Welcome to the great big wonderful world of Big Time Radio. Welcome to WRTP, anyway." He dropped all his stuff on the console and glanced at me.

"And who's this adorable creature?" His voice grew positively suave. He probably spoke that way to every female, but a little sweet-talking was welcome after a barrage of putdowns.

"That's Joey Merino," Peter said. "Joey, Dave Dayton. She's going to be my guest star on the first program."

Dave eyed me up and down. "What a shame this isn't television," he said. "A girl like this should be seen—"

"And not heard," Peter said. Let him have his little joke.

"What do you do, honey?"

"I'm a comedian," I said. "But don't take a poll in here. They'll tell you I'm a pest."

"Well you can pester me anytime you want," he oozed.

I modestly lowered my eyelashes. I tried to blush.

"Uh, Dave?" Peter said. "You have to go on in half an hour. Shouldn't we get started?"

"Oh, let the man talk!" I said. Dave Dayton laughed. Peter looked exasperated. Fred gazed heavenward, as if seeking divine guidance—or a lightning bolt with my name on it.

Was Dave Dayton's put-on come-on making Peter uncomfortable? Even a tad jealous? If only Dave's attention would finally make Peter realize that not only was I witty and talented, but incredibly desirable to boot.

Oh, give up, Joey. None of the above was true. But having Dave Dayton come on to me was a nifty way to kill a few minutes.

For the next half hour he explained the switches and the phone system we'd be using. Peter looked more

40

and more at home in front of the console. I guess he began to remember all the things he already knew.

Dave kept checking to make sure I understood everything too. This irritated Peter. "I'm the one who has to know this. Don't worry about Joey."

We stayed to listen to the first half hour of Dave's show. By that time Peter's confidence had returned.

No thanks to me of course.

Peter wasn't exactly bursting with gratitude as we left the studio. "You know," he said, as we headed upstairs to his uncle's office, "I'm surprised at you. I never thought you were the kind of a girl who would fall for a phony line like Dayton's."

"I'm not," I said casually. "But sometimes junk food is better than no food at all."

Four

I'd known Charlie Bliss almost as long as I'd known Peter, so no introductions were needed. Our talk went smoothly enough. He discussed FCC regulations, slander and libel laws, obscenity, profanity, and the importance of doing the commercials on time.

"What it all boils down to," he said, "is simply a matter of judgment and good taste."

"Good taste is my byword," I declared. "Also punctuality. Of course, I can't speak for Peter."

"I have great confidence in Peter," Mr. Bliss said proudly. "Otherwise I never would have asked him to do the show."

Peter's chest puffed out a little.

When Peter's dad left, Mr. Bliss tried his best to substitute for him, and his best was awfully good. He took Peter to everything from circuses to hockey games.

Camping, fishing, boating; you name it, he took Peter to it.

When Peter decided that where he wanted to go most was to WRTP, Mr. Bliss practically gave him the run of the building.

Not only was Peter's uncle indulgent, he was rich. Or at least reasonably loaded. I don't know how he made his fortune. Certainly not from the radio station. That started as sort of a hobby. He grew to enjoy it so much that he now concentrated on RTP full time.

When Peter was sixteen, Uncle Charlie bought him a Mercury Lynx and enrolled him in a driving school, because he wanted Peter to have more individual road training than he'd get in a high school driver-ed course.

Peter's mother did okay in her real estate business, but as she always says, it has its ups and downs. There were a lot of things Peter wouldn't be able to have or do if it weren't for his uncle.

But probably the best thing about Uncle Charlie is that he thinks Peter is great, which may be more important than all the bread and circuses he provided.

It was pretty late by the time we left. We were supposed to go through the record library and pick out some music for the show, and Peter still had to learn how to fill out a program log—an official one, not our little batch of looseleaf notes.

"It's after six," he said. "I don't even know if anybody will be in the library now. You'd better do it tomorrow."

43

We walked out to the parking lot. "I'll do the log while you're at the library."

I strapped myself into the seat belt. "You know, I'm getting really excited. I mean, it's like I didn't believe it till today, when we were right there in the studio. I guess I didn't think you'd really let me on the show. You keep talking like you're going to ditch me at any minute."

"That's because of the way you keep talking," he said.

"I'm talking the way I always talk. But you're so *grouchy.* Nerves, I guess."

"I guess."

"Aren't you excited too?" I asked. "I swear, if I wasn't in this straitjacket I'd be bouncing up and down and going 'Oohh! Oohh!'"

"You can still go 'oohh oohh,'" he pointed out, "even in your seat belt."

"But how come *you're* not going 'oohh, oohh'?" I asked curiously.

"I am—on the inside. But everything is so last-minute. I wish I had another week to prepare."

"Fiddle de dee," I said. "You've been prepared for years. You'll be great. And *I* am going to make show biz history."

"One way or the other," Peter agreed.

I spent that night polishing up my routines. I'd been working on a new one, but I didn't think it would be ready in time for Saturday's show.

I drove my family crazy as I got more and more hyper, reminding them every hour to listen to me on Saturday, and quizzing them on the hour and the station the program was on.

"You *will* listen, Daddy? You *promise!*"

"Of course I'll listen! Wild horses couldn't keep me away."

"I hope they can keep you awake. You know our show's on at midnight." My father falls asleep at eleven o'clock every night—no matter what.

"I'll keep him awake," my mother said.

"You'll listen, Matt?"

"I told you sixteen times I would. I already warned Monique to prepare for a dull evening."

"Andy, don't forget to listen Saturday night. WRTP. 1301 on your AM dial."

"Radio tripe," he said. "How could I forget? Unfortunately, I'm not allowed to stay up till two."

"I'll make an exception," my mother said.

"Do you have to?" he muttered.

As I tried to fall asleep that night, I pictured how it would be Saturday, with no one in the studio but Peter and me.

We'd be alone, just the two of us. At the witching hour, huddled together over a microphone, alone in the night world, and together in our aloneness. (Except, of course, for the agent who would be listening and discover me.)

This, I thought, is a situation with real potential.

45

We'd have no one to rely on but each other, and who knows what might happen in two hours of such intimacy?

Oh, give up already! I told myself. You relied on each other for years and look what's happened. One kiss, followed by total rejection.

But this could be different. I could see the two of us, at midnight, working side by side, united in a heroic struggle to keep our listeners awake.

I could see Peter turn to me—during a news break, for instance—and say, "I never could have done this without you, Joey. In fact... I can't do anything without you. Can't you see what I'm trying to tell you? I *love* you."

S-u-u-u-r-e that could happen. And at this very moment, the temperature in Hell might be plummeting toward 32°.

I was a dynamo in school the next day. I sprinted to all of my classes so I'd have time to chalk the time of the show on the blackboard, right under where the teachers write "Homework Assignment. Do not erase."

I reminded everyone I saw to listen. Everyone I told already knew about it. I'd been talking it up since Tuesday.

I did such a good job of spreading the word that I figured if the unthinkable happened, and I didn't become a famous comedian, I'd make a dandy PR person.

*   *   *

46

"Take my car," Peter said when he met me that afternoon. He dug into his pocket and tossed me the keys. "You remember where it's parked."

"But aren't you going with me? You have to do the log."

"I'm going to see Fred at seven," he said. "Bring the car back at six-thirty and I'll drive you home and go on to the station."

"Don't you want to pick out the records with me? It's your show."

"I have some other things I have to take care of," he said vaguely. "You can handle the music. It was your idea anyway."

Why didn't Peter want to check on the records I'd select, when he was so possessive about his show? You'd think he'd want to know what he was playing before he put it on the air.

But he just shut his locker door and strolled off down the hall, whistling.

Peter never whistles.

There seemed to be a spring in his step, as if he didn't have a care in the world. I wondered what details he had to take care of, and why he was so cheerful about them. Last night he was wishing he had another week to get ready, yet now, as he walked away from me, there was a jaunty air about him that I'd never seen when he was calm.

I shook my head. Mysterioso, I thought. Extremely mysterioso.

* * *

Gretchen Hackler ran the WRTP record library. She gave me a computer list of everything in RTP's collection, broken down by various categories.

I picked records by their names. I went for the oldies, and the sillier the title sounded, the better. My concept was parody, after all, and there were some dusty treasures down there that hadn't been heard since 1922.

It took almost two hours, because I wanted to listen to everything. Gretchen said we had to make sure that the old records were still playable. She said if the audio quality was poor the record would sound even worse over the air.

Didn't Peter know that? I wondered. How could he assume I knew it? I guess he counted on Gretchen to guide me.

I found some gems. I chose Tiny Tim's version of "Tiptoe Through the Tulips" for our theme music, because it had the antique sound I was aiming at even though it was a modern recording.

At least Peter ought to okay his theme music, I thought. We'd never talked about having a theme song for the show. I had to make the decision myself and hope he'd be satisfied. Where was he? I wondered. What was he doing that was more important than this?

I made all the music decisions, simply following my instincts. I pulled titles like, "I Found a Peach in Orange, New Jersey, in Apple Blossom Time" and "The Girl on the Police Gazette."

Gretchen had giggling fits as we played some of the songs. "I had no idea this stuff was still here. I'm tempted to put some of it on tape and send it down to the night people marked 'Manilow' and 'Streisand.' Can you picture Dakota Stone doing her sensuous-woman intro to "Love Story" and then cueing up "Just a Baby's Prayer at Twilight for her Daddy Over There"?

When I thought we had enough records, Gretchen promised to have them all set up in the studio tomorrow night. "I'm glad Peter's getting to go on the air," she said. "It must be a real kick for him."

"For me too," I reminded her. "Will you listen? You might hear me get discovered."

"I'll listen. If you promise not to tell Charlie Bliss who helped you find these records."

Peter was whistling again that evening as he drove his car from his house to my house. Every once in a while he broke into a hum.

I told him about choosing "Tiptoe Through the Tulips" for his theme song.

"Fine," he said.

I told him about the other records I'd picked.

"Sounds good," he said, after every title I mentioned. I wondered if he was hearing a word I was saying.

"So, did you get all those details cleared up?" I asked.

"Yep."

"Any problems?"

"Nope."

"You're in an awfully good mood," I said suspiciously.

"Yep."

"Listen, I already ate, so I can go to meet Fred with you. I have the list of records and you'll need that for the log—"

"Nope."

"But Peter, you do need—"

He stopped the car in front of my house. I unbuckled my seat belt.

"I'll get them tomorrow night as I play them." He patted my shoulder. "You just work like a little beaver on your monologue tonight. Remember, by Sunday you might be famous. By Sunday we might all be famous."

"*All?* What do you mean, all?" I held on to the half-open car door, one foot on the curb and the rest of me still in the car.

"I'll pick you up tomorrow about eleven. See you."

He gunned the engine like he was going to take off, with the door hanging open and me hanging on to the door.

I jumped out before I was dragged to my death.

"What do you mean, *all of us?*" I repeated. "You know, you're acting really—"

He leaned over and pulled the door shut. "Take care!" he yelled, and sped away in a cloud of intrigue.

"—really bizarre!" I shouted after him.

All of us were going to be famous?

But there'd be no one in the place except him and me. He must have meant both of us.

Just a slip of the tongue. Maybe he meant me, himself, and WRTP. Sure. That's what he meant.

But I lingered on the sidewalk, not sure at all.

Some weird changes were going on inside Peter's

50

head. All of a sudden he was becoming unpredictable. Not only that, he was patronizing me, treating me like a child, bossing me around.

"You just work like a little beaver on your monologue." He'd patted my shoulder exactly the way I pat Andy's when I'm treating him like a little brother.

What was happening to him?

Why did I get the feeling that his sudden blithe spirit was not entirely because we were making our radio debut tomorrow?

Why wasn't he nervous anymore? How come I was standing out here in the cold instead of calming him down, cheering him up, boosting his ego and assuring him that he was going to be great? Why didn't he need me to do that?

And who was "all of us"?

Five

I was so tense and excited on Saturday that I began to think *I* was overrehearsed. I could deliver an hour of comedy, and all Peter wanted was seven minutes. I planned to do my routine on self-improvement books, so I really didn't have to keep going over and over the five other monologues I kept rehearsing.

I thought it would be a good idea to forget about the show for a while and try to relax. Just stretch out on my bed and be still.

I closed my eyes and pictured a lush tropical island. I saw myself lying on the beach in the sun. I listened to the gentle lap of the waves and watched palm trees swaying in the soft, warm breeze. I cleared my mind of everything but the feel of the sun and the sound of the water.

Suddenly someone loomed over me, casting a shadow across my face.

A stranger in Paradise, I thought irritably. I tried to erase him from the picture. But he wouldn't go away.

"We're alone here, you know. Just the two of us." Peter sat down beside me.

"Go away," I said. "This is my island. I don't want to think about you."

"But you *are* thinking about me. You can't help it."

"We're just good friends."

"We're more than that, Joey. Much more." He pulled me into his arms and kissed me the way I had kissed him in his kitchen.

"This is not making me relaxed!" I didn't know if I was saying it to him or to myself.

"I'm not trying to relax you." He nibbled on my ear.

"Good grief!" I sat bolt upright as the palm trees blew away and the ocean dried up. Peter disappeared too, just before I could kick sand in his face.

Ridiculous, I told myself. This is a boy who has to pretend I never kissed him, who's so embarrassed about it that he can't bring himself to ask me why I'd kissed him.

An unbiased observer might point out that I never had the nerve to ask him why he'd invited me to kiss him, but there was no unbiased observer around.

Grow up, already! It'll never happen. Peter is not going to turn to me in the studio tonight and say what I've been waiting for him to say.

And when we went to college together next year would I still be waiting to hear it?

I hadn't exactly spent every minute of high school simply waiting, even though it sometimes felt that way. I have short brown hair, good skin, sparkly eyes, and nice curves. (And maybe chubby cheeks.) There are guys who think I'm "cute." All right, there are some guys who don't think I'm that cute. Not everyone appreciates my lightning wit. But who wants a man with no sense of humor?

I don't know whether I started seeing other boys because I wanted to make Peter jealous, or if I hoped that he'd wake up when he saw that males found me attractive. I did get awfully frustrated sometimes.

From time to time I looked for someone who would turn me on, someone who would give me the sweet kisses and pleasant dreams that Peter never gave me.

Wayne Newberger came close, but after a few steamy sessions in his car, I realized that the only attraction I felt for Wayne was when he kissed me. And Wayne, who had practiced his talent for making out the way I practiced my comedy, couldn't understand what was wrong with that.

"You're boring, Wayne," I said during our final wrestling match. "You take me bowling, which bores me, you take me to boring movies, we have boring conversations—"

"So we'll cut out all the preliminaries," he said, "and get right to the main event. That's what you really want anyway."

"That's just the point." I pushed him away. "That's why we're going to say byebye."

"But that doesn't make any sense!" he argued. "You need loving, you need kissing, you need someone like me."

What I *didn't* need was for Wayne to know it.

"Hey, come on, honey." He pulled me close and gave me a long, slow, skillful kiss, during which I wasn't the least bit bored.

"Your lips were made for kissing," he said, putting his fingers lightly on my mouth. The cliché strengthened my weakening resolve.

"Also for spitting, screaming and biting," I told him. "Take me home before I do something we both regret."

"Oh, do it, baby. You won't regret it."

So I bit his finger.

He howled in outrage.

"You're right," I said. "I don't regret it."

He took me home. Oddly enough, he called me at least five times after that before he took no for an answer.

Peter would ask me very casually about my dates, but he acted pretty indifferent until I started going out with Wayne.

I kept hoping to get a rise out of him, for him to respond to the titillating tidbits I was letting him drag out of me. But all he ever did was nod or grunt or make some comment about Wayne's reputation. He never went any further than that, and I suppose it was just a sort of narrowing of his eyes when I described our dates that made me think he might be a little disturbed about Wayne.

That was last spring. After Wayne, I gave up the search.

But now, I wondered, who knew how Peter would react to anything? He'd suddenly become unpredictable. He yelled at me at the drop of a hat, acted mysterious and secretive, and had taken up whistling.

Was it possible that that very kiss he wouldn't talk about had turned him around? Maybe when I kissed him he finally realized his own appeal, which raised his self-esteem, which bolstered his ego and made him feel more courageous and confident about everything else.

Makes sense, I thought. It would certainly explain why he was so cocky all of a sudden. A passionate kiss from an attractive, hot-blooded person such as myself could be very therapeutic.

Maybe he's grateful to me. Maybe he just can't express it yet. Maybe he needs a bit more confidence before he declares himself.

Wait and see. Wait just a little longer. It's only a few hours till air time, till we're alone in the studio.

All of us?

By the time Peter came to pick me up, I was suffering an intense case of mike fright. I clung to his arm as we walked down the steps to the car. I didn't want him to know that sometime around supper I'd discovered I was a nervous wreck, because part of my job was to make sure that he didn't turn into a nervous wreck.

He didn't seem nervous.

I buckled my seat belt with trembling fingers. "Next stop, Fame and Fortune," I said shakily. "Put the pedal to the metal and steer me to stardom."

"You got it," he said. He snapped his seat belt. "We just have to pick up Dinah."

56

"Dinah? Dinah who?"

All of us.

"Dinah Smythe. She's going to be on the show too."

"Dinah Smythe?" I shrieked. "On our show? You're joking. What's she going to do, read her physics notes?"

Dinah Smythe. Miss Perfect. Blondest hair, bluest eyes, biggest brain. Slim. Serious. Cool. Thin cheeks.

"She's going to sing," Peter replied. "She's pretty good, too. She writes all her own songs."

"Talk about amateur night."

"I promised her you weren't going to make any snide remarks about her singing."

"When did you promise her that?" I demanded. "And when did you discover this budding talent?"

"Yesterday. She auditioned for me."

"Really. And just where did you hold this audition?"

"At her house. When you were at RTP."

"That's why you didn't come with me? *She's* the details you had to take care of?" I wanted to bust out of my seat belt and smack him senseless.

Dinah had been Peter's lab partner in chemistry last year. It was rumored that she had a boyfriend at Columbia—or Yale—or Dartmouth. Every Ivy League college was mentioned in the speculation.

Peter seemed very impressed with her. He talked about how much help she was, and how good at chemistry she was. For a while I thought he might have finally noticed women—but the wrong one. Then, when he didn't talk about her much anymore, I relaxed and figured that his only interest in Dinah was as a lab partner.

57

The puzzle pieces were beginning to fit together.

No wonder I picked out the records by myself. Dinah must have driven him to her house and "auditioned" for him while I was slaving to make his program a success; the only thing he cared about was that I was safely tucked away someplace while he listened to the Ice Princess sing.

Did she really have any talent? With everything else she had going for her, could she sing too? Or did Peter's repressed urges make him tone deaf?

"If she's so good," I said, "why did you have to promise her I wouldn't make any snide remarks about her singing?" I tried to keep my voice steady and my hands away from his throat.

"Well, you have a reputation, Joey. I think she's a little intimidated by you. But I told her there's no reason to laugh—I mean, once I heard her sing—"

"Amazing," I said. "Yesterday the audition, today the show. Talk about your overnight success."

"Yeah, I know all about your long years of struggle and heartbreak." Peter grinned.

You don't know *anything* about heartbreak, buster. *Not thing one.*

"I am a known quantity," I said icily. "You're familiar with my capabilities."

"I'm familiar with Dinah's too."

"Just how familiar did you get?"

"Joey!"

"Stop me if I'm wrong," I began, "but do I sense sex rearing its ugly head?"

Peter hit the accelerator and aimed the Lynx toward the corner. He took a screeching right like he'd never had a driving lesson in his life.

"Why are you doing this to me?" he demanded. "Why now? I go on the air in less than—"

"Because you just told me now!" I yelled. "We planned this whole show together. Don't you think I have a right to find out when you change plans at the last minute? How am I supposed to know what—"

He jammed on the brake. If I hadn't been wearing that stupid seat belt I might have gone straight through the windshield.

"Well, you know now, okay?" His face was dark with anger. *"Okay, Joey?"*

I didn't say anything. I couldn't. I just stared out the window.

"And you know what else? Get off my case! I've really had it. I don't need your sarcasm—"

"You don't need me at all," I said. I kept my face toward the side window, so if the tears in my eyes started to run down my cheeks he wouldn't see them.

What a fool I was. Had enough, Joey? Give up?

"We're going to pick up Dinah, you're going to be nice to her, and you're not going to give me any more grief. Okay?" He shook my shoulder. *"Okay?"*

I knocked his hand away. "Okay. Pick up Dinah, be nice, no more grief. Check. I wouldn't dream of spoiling this power trip you're on."

"Fine."

He shifted into first and we started off again.

"Do you want me to sit in the back so she can sit next to you?" I don't know what masochistic impulse made me say that.

"Don't worry about it," Peter said. "I'm sure Dinah won't mind taking the back seat."

"That'll be a first."

I had a feeling there were going to be a lot of firsts tonight. And maybe some lasts.

Dinah was waiting as we pulled up around her circular driveway. She was carrying a guitar and a bulging folder, which must have contained all the songs she'd ever written.

How many songs was she going to sing? How much air time was Peter going to give her? With an extra person on the show, there would be less time for me.

He's leaving me with nothing, I thought. He's taking it all away—his friendship, his love—and now he's threatening the only thing I have left. My career.

"Hi, Peter," Dinah said breathlessly. "Hi, Joey."

I pushed the car door open. "You want to sit in front?"

"That's okay." Dinah shoved the front seat forward and I bent over like a stapler. My chin nearly hit the dashboard. "There's more room for my guitar and everything back here. I'm so nervous. Are you nervous?"

"I'm doubled over with tension." I straightened up, snapping the seat back into position. I slammed the door.

So Miss Cool was nervous, was she? Another first. And she was intimidated by me. Fine. Terrific. I'm going

60

to get as much time as I need, I vowed, even if I have to intimidate her right out of the studio.

I'm going to knock 'em dead in my first and last radio performance, and if I knock a couple of other performers dead in the process, tough. That's show biz.

Six

Somewhere in the middle of this trauma I lost my mike fright. Maybe a broken heart makes you immune from other emotional strains, or maybe knowing that my career would now be the entire focus of my energies gave me strength.

I sat at one end of the console, with Peter in the middle and Dinah at the other end. They were doing the white-knuckle bit. I psyched myself up by sliding off my chair in a fake faint, pretending to hang myself, and muttering frantic prayers to Jehovah, Allah, Osiris, and Zeus.

"Hedging my bets," I explained. "One of them has to be listening."

At five minutes to air time I began to hum. I patted the pile of commercials I was supposed to hand Peter during the show and contemplated Dinah.

Her face was practically white. The only color in her was a tinge of green around her lips. Dinah Smythe looked like she was about to throw up. I hoped she would. Nothing can kill a budding romance faster than throwing up all over your boyfriend.

"So," I said brightly, "you're going to sing. What an opportunity for you. I mean, even if we don't get fifty thousand listeners—"

Dinah began to look greener.

"I never dreamed you were a singer," I went on. "Let alone a songwriter. I guess this is the first time you ever sang in public, isn't it? I mean, you were never in any of the talent shows or anything."

Elroy the engineer took voice levels. Dinah could hardly croak out a word.

Peter looked at her anxiously. I reached across the console and patted her hand. "Don't worry, Dinah. I'm sure you'll do just fine."

I wasn't sure she'd do fine at all. I wasn't sure Peter would be fine. In fact, I hoped he'd be terrible. I wanted him to screw up. I hated him. I hated his new arrogance, his bossiness, his temperamental outbursts....

His starlet.

It wasn't *my* kiss that turned him around. My kiss didn't transform him into this Frankenstein. It was Dinah's kisses—and God knows what else—that had bloated his ego and set him against me. B.D. (before Dinah) he would never have screamed at me the way he had tonight.

Before this week, any time I'd irritated him or an-

63

noyed him, he'd never let loose with more than a mild, "Stuff it, Wiseass." And hardly ever that. He needed me too much to risk a real fight.

Now he didn't need me anymore.

He must have been seeing her all week.

My stomach tightened.

The engineer signaled five seconds.

Peter hunched over the microphone.

Four seconds.

Dinah sat stiffly in her chair, her hands clasped tightly together.

Three seconds.

To hell with Dinah.

Two seconds.

Forget Peter.

One second.

Numero Uno, that's all.

Cue. Red light on. "Tiptoe Through the Tulips...."

I'm scared. I moved my jaw around, mouthing words silently. I wondered if any words would come out when it was my turn to mouth them audibly.

"Hello out there in Radioland, and welcome to the Peter Zero show. That's me, Peter Zero—"

Peter Zero? What happened to Peter Stillman?

Good question.

"—sitting in for vacationing Dakota Stone. We've got some talk, some laughs, and some of the sweetest music this side of the Crimean War. So don't touch that dial! Put your ear to the speaker and let's party!"

He slumped back in his chair with a "whoosh" as the theme music came up. I stared at him. Dinah stared at him. Whoever Peter Zero was, he must have been born with a microphone in his hand.

Music down.

"Yes, folks, it's Peter Zero, and to get us all in the right mood, we've dug deep into WRTP's mighty music archives—and I do mean deep—for this snappy little number called 'Lena from Palesteena.'"

Our mikes were shut while the record played. I couldn't stop staring at him. He was still breathing hard, but his voice was brisk and businesslike. "What comes next?"

"You've got the log," I said. "When did you become Peter Zero?"

He checked the clock on the wall. "About two minutes ago."

Dr. Jekyll and Mr. Hyde, no joke. Joke? It was downright spooky.

"Can I talk?" Dinah whispered.

"Only when the music's on," Peter said. He shuffled through the papers on the console. There were dozens of them.

"Where are the commercials? Joey, those commercials are supposed to be stacked up in order—"

"Calm down," I said. "They're right here someplace with the other stuff."

Peter glanced at the program log. "It's live," he said. "I have to read it. Cockeyed Harry's House of Audio. *Where are the commercials?*"

Cockeyed Harry's House of Audio. That sounded sort of promising. A good way to get my voice warmed up. I kept my elbow on the pile of commercials beside me.

Elroy cued us. The music stopped.

Peter Zero disappeared. Peter Stillman shot me a look of panic, like an animal trapped in the headlights of an oncoming car. I smiled sweetly, lifted my elbow, and picked up the first commercial.

"And now," I said, my voice shaking only a little, "a message from Cockeyed Harry's House of Audio."

Peter's eyes narrowed into mean little slits.

"Yes, friends," I said, "whatever you want in the field of electronics, Cockeyed Harry has it. Audio, video, stereo—"

Peter grabbed the commercial from my hand. How unprofessional, I thought. How petty. Now I'll have to improvise. I felt eerily calm.

"Listen," I ad-libbed, "let's get right to the point. You've seen Cockeyed Harry on television. You know what a fool he looks like. You know he's got to be crazy to sell at these prices. Let me tell you, he's not called Cockeyed Harry for nothing. He bends over backwards so far to make his customers happy he keeps hitting his head on the ground.

"A six-year-old could rob Cockeyed Harry blind. Think of the deals *you* can make. So go to any one of Cockeyed Harry's Long Island stores and grab up some incredible bargains before they have him committed."

I couldn't help beaming as I shoved the stack of commercials toward Peter. I was wonderful! I was dynamite! At this very moment, two Cub Scouts, three pregnant women, an assorted bunch of silly folks, and a famous agent were wondering who that fresh new personality was.

66

Two taped spots followed Cockeyed Harry. Elroy took over.

"Not bad, eh?" I said brightly when our mikes were off.

Peter's face was almost purple with rage.

"I read the commercials, Joey," he said dangerously. "Don't ever do that again."

"I was only trying to help you out of a tight spot," I said innocently. "Like I promised I would. Wasn't I great?"

"I wouldn't have been in a tight spot if you hadn't hidden the commercials. One more stunt like that—"

"But you haven't let me say a word yet," I complained.

"We've only been on for six minutes!" He turned to Dinah and his voice softened into mush. "You'll go on in about half an hour, okay?"

She gulped and clutched her guitar to her chest.

The engineer cued Peter.

"We're back again, Peter Zero and his group of assorted zanies." There he goes again. The guy really is a Jekyll and Hyde. No trace of anger in his voice, no hint that he had just snarled at me like a vicious Doberman, only hearty good cheer and Dave Dayton smoothness.

"Let me introduce my main zany, up-and-coming young comedian Joey Merino. Say hello to the people, Joey."

I leaned toward the mike. "Hello to the people, Joey. That was my Gracie Allen imitation. How am I doing so far? Am I a star yet?"

"Give it a few more minutes," Peter said.

Elroy gestured for me to move back from the mike. I readjusted myself in the chair. My heart thudded now, even though I'd been okay doing the commercial.

This was different. This was me, Joey Merino, with an introduction and everything.

Main zany. He practically said I was his sidekick, his partner, an integral part of the show.

Well... maybe I don't want him to *totally* screw up.

"And our special guest star, the Midnight Warbler, Dinah Smythe."

She, on the other hand, should screw up. Totally.

Midnight Warbler. Special guest star. I was supposed to be the special guest star. If Dinah was special, what did that make me?

Stupid question. Don't think about it.

"Say hi to the folks, Dinah."

Dinah opened her mouth. Nothing came out. She looked frantically at Peter and shook her head.

I smiled smugly at Peter's expression of dismay. Miss Perfect is panicking. Tsk.

He recovered fast. "That's right, save your voice for your singing, Warbler. First we'll play a few more snappy tunes, and then we'll open the phones for a while so you can call in and tell us what's on your mind. Joey and I are going to discuss some controversial issues that concern us all and we want you to join in. From anywhere on Long Island call..."

He was really in his element. All those years of secret practicing, of hanging around the station, of listening to WRTP's personalities had paid off.

Dinah was gazing at him like an awestruck puppy. Were we both seeing this whole new Peter for the first time? Or had she gotten a glimpse of him yesterday, when they—

Don't think about it.

"...dispute about whether vigorous exercise is really good for you. One controversial study even reported that heavy exercise can cause cancer. Do you exercise, Joey?"

"Yes," I said, "but in moderation. I developed a whole workout program for myself. I even created my own exercises. Like, for instance, liebacks."

"Liebacks?" Peter repeated. "Are they anything like sit-ups?"

"They're exactly like sit-ups," I said, "except you don't sit up. You lie on the floor with your arms at your sides, making sure your body is in straight alignment."

"Then what?" asked Peter.

"You repeat that ten times."

"Sounds real challenging." Peter was doing a nice job as a straight man, I thought. We hadn't rehearsed this, but I'd given him a general idea of what I was going to say.

"Then after the liebacks, I do a series of pushdowns," I went on. "They're based on push-ups, but in my exercise you don't work against your body, you work with it."

"How?" Peter asked.

"In pushdowns, you don't push. You lie on your

69

stomach with your head turned to the right. You do a series of those, then you turn your head to the left and do another series of five. You can see that pushdowns are a lot more demanding than liebacks. They require actual movement of a part of the body. You want to go easy on the pushdowns the first few times you exercise."

"No point in overdoing it," Peter agreed.

I imagined my wit crackling over the airwaves like the electricity that powered the radios of all those listeners.

There were six lights on the phone board in front of us. None of the lights was lit. Where was my agent?

"Let me give you our number again in case you missed it," Peter said. "It's real easy: 620-WRTP."

Of course, that's why my agent hadn't phoned yet. He or she hadn't gotten the number the first time.

"We'll get to your calls after our exclusive WRTP newsbreak."

Elroy took over.

Still no lights on the phone board.

"What calls?" I asked. "Nobody's calling."

"I can see that," Peter said.

"We're supposed to stir up the listeners and take phone calls till one o'clock. We never planned what to do if nobody called."

"Maybe Dinah ought to sing now," Peter said.

Dinah jumped up from her chair and walked to the other side of the studio. "I'm not ready yet." She sounded like she was choking. It should only happen.

70

"I could do my monologue," I suggested. "I'm all warmed up."

"No, not now. You've been on for the last fifteen minutes. We'll just have to play another record." Peter pulled off his headphones and stood up. "Look, Dinah, you're going to have to sing sometime. The longer you wait, the harder it's going to be."

"You guys are doing a fine job," she said. "You sound like professionals. I'll just sit and sort of observe for a while."

"The girl's no trouper," I muttered.

Peter glared at me. He walked over to Dinah and took her hand. Then he started speaking softly, lovingly, in a voice I had never heard. "You said you wanted to do this. You said you wanted to find out if you—"

"Well, I can't!" she blurted.

So it was *her* idea to sing on the show. Maybe Peter never planned this at all. Maybe when she heard about the program she'd come looking for him, asking for her shot at fame and fortune.

I couldn't imagine why she needed it. Harvard, yes, grad school, yes, the Rand Corporation, yes, but singing?

Peter rubbed Dinah's shoulders as she sagged back against him.

"You can do it, Dinah. I know you can." He gently massaged the back of her neck. "Just sing like you sang for me."

I tried to look away. I didn't want to see them, didn't want to hear Peter murmuring this way, his hands stroking Dinah, and Dinah turning to look at him, her big blue eyes wide and pleading.

But I couldn't stop looking. I must have a morbid streak, I thought, because I can't turn my back on them, and seeing them like this makes me shrivel up inside.

"Oh, grow up, Dinah," I said finally. "What are you so afraid of? You're going to be valedictorian and talk in front of five hundred people at graduation."

"That's different," she said.

"Yeah. Then you'll have an audience." I pointed to the phone board. *"Nobody's listening.* Even if you sing like a buffalo in heat, no one's going to hear you. So why don't you just pick up your guitar and come over here and stop giving Peter all this grief?"

At least I broke up their love scene. I hoped Peter recognized that I was not the only one giving him grief. And if there was any justice, Dinah *would* sing like a buffalo in heat.

"Elroy's signaling, Peter," I said. "If you two can tear yourselves away from each other."

I knew I shouldn't have said it, but I couldn't hold back. And now that I called them "you two," I was admitting that they had a special relationship that excluded me.

I sounded sarcastic and jealous. I couldn't help it. I *was* jealous.

"You be nice, Joey," Peter warned.

"You're being nice enough for both of us."

"Let's go, Dinah," he said firmly. "You're on in five minutes."

72

Seven

Peter played a lively rendition of "They're Wearing 'Em Higher in Hawaii" to open the second half hour of the show. Then he gave Dinah an extravagant introduction, contrasting her "now" sound with our moldy oldies.

I smiled contentedly as Peter tried to engage her in a bit of preliminary chitchat.

I expected her to freeze. She looked as rigid as a T square, but she managed to whisper the name of the song she was going to sing.

I sat back in my chair, my hands folded in my lap, and closed my eyes. If Zeus, Allah, Jehovah, or Osiris was listening, Dinah would make a fool of herself, and Peter Zero too.

I grinned as Dinah trembled her way through the first two lines of her song. Dinah's voice stopped trembling. I stopped grinning. I opened my eyes and stared.

73

She didn't sound like a buffalo in heat. She sounded like a perfectly adequate folk singer, with a clear, true voice and a sincere delivery.

Her lyrics didn't stink either.

Zeus, Allah, Jehovah, and Osiris must be out to lunch.

Peter beamed at her like a proud father at a ballet rehearsal. When she finished, he started to clap. I just sat there, grim-faced, until Peter shot me a pointed look.

So I clapped too. Slowly. Reluctantly. Elroy the engineer clapped from behind his glass booth. Had Elroy clapped for me? Do not ask for whom Elroy clapped....

"Beautiful, Dinah, just beautiful!" Peter raved. "You can hear the response of our vast studio audience. Listen to the cheers."

."Cheer," I said sourly.

Dinah looked drained.

"We'll hear more of Dinah Smythe and her original songs right after this word from Big Al's Auto Body."

Peter read the commercial and then cut to pre-recorded public service spots. I leaned over and sank my nails into his wrist—only deep enough to draw blood.

"Just how much more are we going to hear of her?" I whispered.

He pried my nails out of his wrist. "You leave that up to me. Don't be jealous. I know how you hate to share the spotlight, but—"

Is that all he thought it was?

"I'm not good at sharing anything," I said.

"Was I all right, Joey?" Dinah asked. "What did you think?"

"The vast studio audience loved you," I said.

She grinned proudly.

And sang two more songs.

Almost an hour of the show was gone and my agent hadn't called. Peter was partly right; professional jealousy was one of the reasons for my bad temper. That, and the tight, icy knot in my stomach.

When Dinah finally finished humming and strumming we cut to a taped Consumerflash.

"When do I get to do my routine?" I demanded. "Or are you guys going to do the rest of this show alone?"

The one thing Peter hadn't listed in the log was when I would be on. He said we'd wait for a dull spot and put me in there.

"Peter, look!" Dinah pointed to the phone board. Two lights flashed cheerily.

Peter lunged for the mike. "Elroy, put us on delay! Girls, get your headphones on. We're going right to the phones."

"Peter! When do I—"

"Shh! We're on." Peter punched one of the buttons on the board. "Hello! You're on the air."

"Howdy. Just wanted to tell you I enjoyed the little gal's singin'."

I thought Dinah's eyes were going to pop out of her head. If they didn't pop out on their own, I'd be glad to help.

I contemplated shoving their microphones down their

throats and hijacking the show. After my takeover, which I could stage during the next newsbreak, I'd have a whole hour of the Peter Zero show to myself. I could do all eight of my routines.

"I used to do a little singin' myself," the caller went on. "But you probably never heard of me. That was before your time."

I hoped I could keep the anger out of my voice as I grabbed the mike. "You think you're playing with children here?" I said. "I'll bet I've heard of you."

Elroy gestured for me to let go of the mike and sit back.

"You sound like a cowboy," Peter said. "I guess you're not from around these parts."

I thought about grabbing Peter's microphone, but I'd scheduled the coup d'état for one A.M. I could wait five minutes.

"I'm just here visitin' my daughter. I used to be a cowboy. Fact is, I was the last of the singin' cowboys."

"Why the last?" Peter asked.

"I got my start in show business right after the war. World War II. You know about that?"

"We've heard rumors of it," I said.

"Singin' cowboys were goin' out of style. Wasn't much work for us. Mostly they were makin' pictures about tap-dancin' sailors and boozy private eyes."

Two more lights were flashing on the switchboard.

"You still haven't told us your name," Dinah said.

What was Dinah doing talking into a microphone? Had Peter jabbed her with a cattle prod?

He looked startled. And pleased. I can imagine what I looked like.

"Bronco Billy Bell," the caller said. "Ever hear of me?"

"Sure," I lied. "I think I've seen a couple of your movies." Well, I'd told him I'd know who he was. It would have been cruel to disappoint the man.

All the phone lines were lit up.

"I hate to say goodbye, Bronco Billy," Peter said, "but it's time for the news. Call us back next week. Maybe you can sing a song for us."

Oh, dandy. Another Warbler.

"Okey doke. Ride 'em easy."

Elroy took over.

"Wasn't he interesting?" Dinah said. "I hope he calls back next week."

Sure. So he can praise your adequate singing again.

"Maybe I should have asked him to be a guest," Peter said. "Look at those phones."

"Just what we need," I said. "*Another* guest. How come the phones didn't start ringing until he called? Aren't we supposed to be the stars here?"

And there's already one more of "we" than we need.

"He's good radio," Peter said. "And he's got a lot of people calling, which was the whole idea."

"That wasn't *my* idea! My idea was to get my act together and put it on the air!"

"You will," he said mildly. "We have another hour to go."

"Nobody will be listening by then! At least now we know there are six people out there."

"Don't be a prima donna. You'll work the phones with me. You too, Dinah, if you want. Just jump right in."

I'll kill him. I'll kill her. Didn't I schedule the revolution for this break?

"And we'll get to your monologue when we finish with the phone calls."

"Will that be before or after we go off the air?" I asked. I meant it sarcastically, but Jeanne Dixon couldn't have called it better.

The phones went berserk after the news:

"Hey, you know there's a Bronco Billy movie on next week? *Trouble on the Pecos.*"

"He sure brings back a lot of memories.... It was just after the war—forty-six, no maybe forty-seven—and we were living in this little apartment...."

"Hey, Dinah, I never knew you could sing! Way to go! Hi, Joey."

And so it went.

A lot of kids from school called to gush over Dinah's singing. They were all surprised by her secret songwriting. Nobody gushed over me. What was there to gush about? The kids already knew I was funny; the only surprising thing about me was that I'd hardly opened my mouth for the last half hour.

At nine minutes to two, Peter introduced me. "And now, for our really big finish, here's that hilarious new comedienne, Joey Merino!"

By this time I was almost speechless with rage. I wished I'd croaked them both at one A.M., like I'd planned. Sure, I'd "bantered" with the callers, but the callers did most of the talking.

Peter had kept saying, "This is good radio," every time I nagged for my share of air.

"Good for who?" I'd long since stopped marveling at the dynamic new Peter Zero. All I felt now was that I'd been betrayed and abandoned.

Peter had forgotten all about me. He'd ignored me. He'd broken his promise to me—or almost had. The phone board was dark as I faced the microphone for my solo.

I faced everything solo, I realized. Peter simply didn't give a hoot about me anymore.

I felt like an overwound clock. I took a deep breath and tried to convert my anger and frustration into positive energy, using those emotions to come on strong and snappy.

I didn't want to do the riches-to-rags story I'd planned on. It was too self-deprecating and I'd been put down enough already.

So at the last minute I switched to my blind-date routine.

I thought I sounded a little harsh, like I was trying too hard, as if my real feelings were showing through the comic façade. But Peter and Dinah laughed in the right places—even though Peter knew the sketch— and that encouraged me.

Eventually I began to relax and cool down a little. I launched into my description of Albert the undertaker and his bizarre courting rituals. Now I was really on track. I was just working up to the grand finale when Peter shoved a note in front of me.

"*Late. Cut it.*"

I felt like he'd hit me with a hammer. Somehow I finished my sentence. Then, stunned, I turned to him. There were two minutes left in the routine.

"What a story!" he said. "We're going to have to keep you in suspense, folks, because we've just run out of time. That's a wrap for this installment of the Peter Zero show. Tune in next Saturday for more thrilling entertainment with my guest stars, Tom Selleck, Dan Rather, Paul McCartney and Joan Collins."

Cue "Tiptoe Through the Tulips."

The ON THE AIR sign went dark. Peter yanked off his headphones and leaped out of his chair. "Fantastic!" he shouted. "*Fan*-tastic!"

"You were wonderful," Dinah said. "You both were."

I couldn't move.

Peter pulled my headphones off. "We were all wonderful."

"You cut me off." I could hardly get the words out.

Peter pulled me from the chair. "Come on, Joey, you were great. We just ran out of time." He grabbed Dinah's arm. "*You* were great. I knew you could do it." He hugged her.

I was so cold I was numb. Didn't Peter realize what he'd done to me?

"You cut me off," I repeated loudly. "You cut me off before I finished."

"I'm sorry, Joey. You had your seven minutes." He and Dinah stopped hugging. They locked arms. "You

80

didn't tell me you were switching routines. This one was too long."

"If you had let me go on earlier," I said, "it wouldn't have mattered."

"Joey, this is a great moment for me. This is probably the greatest moment in my life. Why do you want to ruin it?"

"Ruin it?" I shrieked. Now I *was* going to cry. How could he be so selfish, so stupid, so insensitive? "This was supposed to be the greatest moment in my life too! My big break. My golden opportunity. Don't you understand what you did to me?"

"I couldn't help it," he insisted. "You changed plans on me at the last minute."

"*I* changed plans on *you?*" I raged. "What about your last-minute guest star?"

Dinah's face clouded over.

"Let's get out of here," Peter said tiredly. "I thought we could all celebrate or something, but if you're not in the mood...."

I struggled to lower my voice, to tone down my hysteria.

"Just tell me, Peter *Zero*, just tell me one thing I ought to celebrate."

Eight

Peter drove me home first. Naturally. As soon as he dumped the third wheel, he could have an intimate little celebration with his Midnight Warbler.

"I'll walk you to the door," he said as we stopped in my driveway.

"Don't bother. I can manage to make it to the house by myself."

"You sound just like Miss Piggy when you talk like that," he said. He came around to my side of the car and opened the door.

"Thank you very much. I'll add that compliment to the list of other nice things you did to me tonight."

I walked ahead of him up the driveway.

"Joey, come on," he coaxed. "You were good. Really good."

"How could you tell? How could *anybody* tell?"

We stood at my front door and I fumbled around in my purse for the key.

"You're overreacting. I know you resented Dinah's singing, but—"

"Peter, go to hell. I don't want to talk to you anymore, I don't want to see you anymore. If you're too stupid to see how you shafted me—"

"I didn't mean to! We just ran out of time. I'll make it up to you. You can do two monologues next week."

"Next week?" I stopped searching for my key and examined his face in the dim light from the porch lantern. "What do you mean, next week?"

"I want you to be on the show again. You're good. Your exercise bit was great. I think you're a natural."

"Is Dinah going to be on again too?" I asked.

"If she wants to. Come on, Joey, we're a great team. Remember?"

Oh sure. Just the three of us. Ham and eggs and Spam. Spic 'n' Span 'n' Spot. Romeo and Juliet and Bozo the Clown.

"Can't you find your key in there?" He reached for my bag.

I held it away from him. "Don't worry. I'll find it. You don't want to keep your warbler waiting."

"Will you do the show? I promise, you'll get twenty minutes all to yourself. No matter how many phone calls we get. Ten minutes each hour. I know you're a little miffed now, but—"

"You're so observant, Peter." A *little* miffed? If I was any miffed-er I'd be chewing on the doorknob. I found the key.

A second chance was so unexpected, though, I didn't know what to say. If I had to go through another two hours watching Peter drool over his protégée, feeling my heart sink like a brick in a bathtub, I wasn't sure I could stand it.

"I'll let you know."

"I really need you, Joey."

"For what?" I unlocked the door and stepped inside.

"For a lot of things."

I wanted to believe him. I wanted so badly to believe him. But just then he glanced at his car, as if to reassure himself that Blonde Beauty was still there, waiting for him to drive her off into the sunrise for some celebratory snuggling.

"Not anymore you don't," I said. "All your needs are being fulfilled just fine. In fact, you're fulfilling needs I never even knew you had."

He looked totally mystified as I closed the door in his face.

April Abruzzo called at nine-thirty Sunday morning, bubbling over with compliments. This annoyed Matt and Andy no end, since even when they're not awake till two-thirty on a Saturday night, they never roll out of bed on a weekend until noon. At the earliest.

I don't know what April was doing up so early either, since she hasn't spent a Saturday night at home since seventh grade. But April's call was only the beginning.

The fourth time the phone rang, Matt and Andy charged into my room like uncaged lions and threatened to strangle me with the phone cord.

"But everybody wants to congratulate me!" I said. "They're telling me how fantastic I was."

"One more call," Matt said menacingly, "and I'll tell them you're dead."

"And you will be," Andy added.

"Don't be dumb. Just unplug your phones. I'll get the calls. Isn't it incredible how your mood can improve when a new day dawns?"

"I don't know," Matt snarled. "When day dawns I try to sleep through it."

"You're sick," Andy said to me. "You're very sick."

"Just pull your plugs," I said cheerfully, "and hop into your little beds and drift back to dreamland."

"Can I hit her?" Andy asked Matt.

"Better not. She's cracked already."

I bounced out of bed as they stumbled off. It was amazing how different I felt this morning after four kids from school had each spent almost ten minutes shouting superlatives into my ear. My family had been waiting up for me last night, but I was too miserable to listen to their dutiful praise.

Now my black depression was doing a complete one-eighty. I pulled on jeans and my "Funny Girl" sweatshirt. Overnight I'd risen from darkest despair to beam like Little Mary Sunshine.

I took my phone downstairs with me and plugged it into the jack in the family room.

It rang again.

"Joey? Charlie Bliss."

"Mr. Bliss! What did you think of the show?"

"That's why I called. You're not the easiest person in the world to reach, you know."

"I know," I said cheerily. "The phone hasn't stopped

85

ringing since nine-thirty. Johnny Carson hasn't called yet, but you're the next best thing. Did you like the show?"

"I loved it. Three fresh new voices—it was a real change of pace for us."

"But how did I do? Was I okay? Did I sound good on the air?"

"Very good. That's the other reason I called. That commercial you did for Cockeyed Harry."

Uh oh. I'd forgotten about tampering with the advertising. "I'm sorry about that," I said. "It's just that Peter lost the copy." I hoped Zeus, Allah, Jehovah, and Osiris were still out to lunch.

He chuckled. "Harry Taubman called me this morning. He loved it. He wants to use your line about bending over backwards and hitting his head on the floor in all his commercials. Not only that, but he wants you to do his spots on the show, and joke it up as much as you want. He thinks you're a riot."

"Who am I to argue with a sponsor?" I giggled as I thought of how Peter insisted that he was the only one allowed to read commercials on his show. I tried to imagine what his reaction had been when Uncle Charlie told him that Cockeyed Harry wanted me to do his ads.

But I didn't even know if I would do the show again. "Three fresh new voices." All of us. That thought was enough to cast a thundercloud over Little Mary Sunshine.

I have to admit I was pretty impressed. Cockeyed

Harry himself had gotten up at the crack of dawn to call Mr. Bliss about me.

And Peter had promised me two routines—twenty whole minutes to myself. But was that enough compensation for the other hundred minutes I'd have to spend in the studio?

I spent the rest of Sunday in quiet contemplation of my life—in between phone calls. The first question on my list of things to contemplate was whether I'd do the Peter Zero show next week. But I think I'd made up my mind within five minutes of speaking to April.

If all these people thought I was so good before they even heard what I could do, then imagine the response when I really got a chance to show my stuff.

Even if I had to watch Peter and Dinah ogle each other for two hours, even if they made me feel like the third person on a bicycle built for two, at least I wouldn't be treated that way on the air.

And if my stomach clenched and my heart felt like lead every time they touched each other, well, that's show biz. There's probably a broken heart for every mike in broadcasting. I'm going into a tough business. The sooner I get tough, the better.

I'd ignore them. Laugh, clown, laugh, I reminded myself. While they dissipated their creative energies in a mindless pursuit of physical pleasure, I would sharpen my comic talent, keep my eye on Numero Uno, and let every male over the age of seventeen know I was back in circulation.

Nine

On Monday I felt like the brightest star in Jefferson High's galaxy.

Kids who'd never spoken to me before stopped me to say how much they'd enjoyed me on Peter's show. Friends hugged me and pointed me out to other kids in the halls.

Andy stopped me on my way to English with two girls who just *had* to meet me. "My sister," he announced. He sounded almost proud.

There was scattered applause as I walked into my classes, and Mrs. Altman, my homeroom teacher, jokingly asked for my autograph.

And everybody asked me to tell them the end of my Albert the undertaker story. "Be sure and mention that to Peter," I said.

I've heard that stars like Paul Newman and Dustin

Hoffman and Woody Allen complain that they never have any privacy and get really irritated when people pester them for autographs.

I myself was not irritated.

Just before lunch, Peter met me at my locker. He was wearing his jacket.

"Ready to go?" he said.

"Go where?"

"McDonald's. It's Monday, remember?"

"Oh, right. Fish sticks." I reached for my jacket.

This was the second surprise of the day. The first was when he came to drive me to school, as if I'd never told him I didn't want to see him again.

I was gracious about it. I had my priorities in order.

We talked about the show, and the phone calls we'd gotten, and how pleased Uncle Charlie was. Dinah's name never came up. He must have been trying to worm his way back into my good graces so I'd be on the second program, because just before we got to school, he asked if I'd made up my mind yet.

"Cockeyed Harry convinced me," I said. "Thinking up a dopier commercial than the ones he uses was a challenge I couldn't resist."

"Great," Peter said. "I'm sure thinking dopey won't be that big a challenge for you."

Now, with my jacket half on and my books stowed in my locker, I wondered where Dinah was and why her name still hadn't come up.

"We'll go meet Dinah and then we can get going," Peter said.

"Dinah's coming too?"

"Uh, yeah." He looked uncomfortable, like all this pretending that we were still good friends was beginning to be a strain. Like he knew perfectly well that I hated Dinah, but he didn't want to know it.

I pulled my arm out of my jacket and hung the jacket back in my locker. I slammed the door.

"What's the matter?" he asked. "Aren't you coming?"

"You two run along and have a nice time," I said. "I'm sure you can manage without me."

"What's the matter?"

You blind fool. Can't you see what I'm trying to tell you? I *hate* you.

"Nothing's the matter," I said coolly. "I just decided to eat here. I don't want to deprive my public of their chance to fawn over me."

Peter looked thoughtful. "Good point. I don't want to deprive me of being fawned over either. I don't get a whole lot of fawning. We'll stay in too. I'll just go get Dinah."

"I'll see you downstairs."

I tried to dismiss the pain I felt when Peter said *"We'll* stay in." It could be simple hunger pangs.

But I wasn't hungry for fish sticks.

A constant stream of kids flowed by our table all through lunch. I ate up the compliments instead of the fish sticks. It was a great meal.

Dinah seemed flustered by the whole thing.

Amateur.

90

Peter, who had always been invisible in any group larger than four, handled his fans like he was used to having fans.

"Glad you liked it," he'd say, or "Thanks for listening," or "Tune in next week." He was using his Peter Zero voice. In fact, he was using his Peter Zero personality.

Almost everybody wanted to know about Bronco Billy. I was feeling so good I didn't mind too much. After all, he'd only been on for two minutes, and none of the kids had ever heard of him except a few nostalgia freaks.

Toward the end of lunch period, things began to quiet down. Peter turned to Dinah and said, "They *loved* you. Now do you believe me?"

Dinah shook her head helplessly. "This is so strange. I'm not used to—"

At which moment Wayne Newberger's hand dropped on my shoulder.

"Hey, girl, you are really something."

I didn't have to shift into flirt, didn't even have time to flutter my eyelashes, because he slid onto the bench right next to me, never taking his hand off my shoulder.

I was aware that conversation between Peter and Dinah had died. I was also aware that my old chemical reaction to Wayne hadn't.

I tilted my face to look up at him with big, admiring eyes. "Did you think I was good?"

He grinned. "I always thought you were good. But you really showed me something Saturday night."

"What was that?" I asked innocently.

91

My wide-eyed act was total fraud, but with Wayne sitting hip to hip against me, with Wayne's thumb moving toward the back of my neck, there was nothing fake about the tingling in my nerve endings.

"See me this Saturday night and I'll tell you," he said.

"I can't. I'll be doing the show again Saturday."

"Friday then."

"She'll be busy Friday too," Peter cut in.

"Really." Wayne looked over my head at Peter. "With you?"

"We have to work on the show," Peter said.

"All night?"

I tried to keep a straight face. And calm nerve endings. "Gee, Wayne, this is so sudden. Are you sure you want to go out with me for myself alone, or because you get a thrill out of being with a superstar?"

"I always got a thrill out of being with you, Joey," Wayne purred. "I've got the scar to prove it."

Behind me I imagined Peter's face turning purple. It probably wasn't turning purple, but I wanted to think that it was. He knew about my last date with Wayne, knew that I'd had to resort to violence, although I'd left the details sketchy. Wayne was the only boy I dated whom Peter seemed to resent. A little.

"Maybe the week after next?" I asked Wayne.

Wayne squeezed my shoulder. "If I can wait that long."

"Channel your energies into something constructive," I murmured in my Dakota Stone voice. "Build a scale model of me out of Popsicle sticks."

92

I rested my chin on my hands as I watched him walk away from our table. It was a pleasant view.

"Joey, I don't like this."

I tore my eyes away from Wayne's back and regarded Peter with an icy stare. "My private life is none of your business."

He can't be jealous, I thought. Can he?

"I'm talking to you as a friend."

Former friend.

"I just don't want you to get in trouble."

"Don't worry. I can handle myself."

"So can Wayne," he retorted. "He's had practice."

"Joey, he *is* rather notorious," Dinah said. "His role model is Warren Beatty. You don't want to end up as just another notch on his belt."

She sounded almost sincere.

"Your concern is touching," I said. "But in the first place, I don't think there's room on his belt for any more notches. And in the second place, if I want to be a notch, that's my business."

I really wasn't sure I'd go anywhere with Wayne Newberger, week after next or ever. Flirting with him was just Step One in my campaign to advertise that Spic 'n' Span had split.

"I get this feeling," Peter said, "that you're going to do something really stupid, and I don't know why."

He doesn't know why? Talk about stupid. Talk about blind fools. How did he locate Dinah's lips without a road map?

Disgusting thought.

I shrugged. "I'm such a madcap even I don't know what I'm going to do next."

And Peter doesn't have to know either.

Let *him* worry for a change. Let *him* try and figure *me* out for a change.

Oh, grow up, Joey. He's got more interesting things to figure out than you.

Like, how to unfold his road map.

"Bell, Bronco Billy: Nicknamed 'Last of the Singing Cowboys,' he made his final film appearance in Republic's *Song of the Tumbleweed*, which is generally considered to be the last singing cowboy movie made in Hollywood. (1951)

"After minor roles in several non-musical Westerns, Billy retired from show business and opened Bronco Billy's Double Bar-B Dude Ranch in Arizona. He also took a fling at writing *(You Can Uke and Yodel Too)*, selling used cars, and real estate speculation.

"His venture into dog food manufacturing was particularly unfortunate. There was consumer resistance to Bronco Billy's Rangeburgers, made from horsemeat. 'I guess,' Billy said, 'they didn't like the idea of their dog eating what I used to put a saddle on.'

"Currently Bronco Billy is living in relative obscurity with his wife, Edna, in Tucson, Arizona."

I tossed the paperback of *Where Are They Now?* on the floor. "That's downright depressin', pardners. It sounds like he bombed at everything."

We were in my family room—just the three of us—

planning Saturday's show. I was determined to act like Good Old Joey.

"It is sad," Dinah agreed. "To think that phoning a radio program is the closest he's been to show business in thirty-five years."

"He's not obscure now," Peter said. "He's been on the radio and thousands of people have heard him."

"He's been on RTP," I corrected. "He's still obscure. Maybe I'll watch that movie of his tomorrow, so when he calls I can tell him how good he was."

"That's nice, Joey." Peter sounded surprised.

I guess I felt sorry for Bronco Billy. After all, he was near the end of the trail, and I was just saddling up to gallop toward fame and fortune. I could afford a generous gesture.

"Okay, let's get down to business." Peter opened his notebook.

We'd been working for an hour and a half when I excused myself for a quick trip to the bathroom. I wasn't gone for more than two minutes, but when I walked back into the room Peter had his hand on Dinah's hair and his lips an inch from her ear.

I stood frozen for a moment, not able to decide whether I wanted to see what he was about to do, or break it up before he could do anything.

I can figure out what he's going to do, and I don't want to see it, I thought. And the Wayne Newberger gambit isn't working, because no matter what, I end up thinking of Peter, and Peter is thinking about Dinah.

He's not jealous at all. I'm the one that's jealous.

"Oh, hi, Joey!" Dinah said loudly.

Peter let go of Dinah's hair. He looked as if he'd been caught with his hand in the cookie jar, which is a repulsive but appropriate comparison.

"Are we finished for today?" I asked. "Or is this just recess?"

Peter hauled himself off the floor. He reached down to help Dinah to her feet. "I guess we can stop now. We got a lot done."

"Yes. Isn't it amazing," I marveled, "how much you can accomplish in a short time?"

Peter kept driving me to school, but I was convinced that he was obsessed with Dinah, that he spent every waking moment with her and every sleeping moment dreaming about her.

I started eating lunch with Wayne, partly because I couldn't stand watching the two of them drool over each other across the chow mein, and partly because I felt an urgent need for someone to drool over me.

At least for forty-two minutes a day I could almost forget them. At least for forty-two minutes a day somebody gave me his undivided attention.

I worked on a new routine and I prepared a commercial for Cockeyed Harry.

By Friday it had gotten pretty hard for Good Old Joey to laugh it up. We were all being extremely polite. Dinah and I were icily formal to each other. Peter and I discussed nothing but his program. He ignored my occasional sarcastic comment and I tried to ignore the

96

gloppy sentiment in his voice whenever he spoke to Dinah.

After the show, I told myself, I won't have to listen to Peter's voice anymore. I won't have to see them together, won't have to feel like a despised chaperone hovering over the young lovers while they conspire to wangle some privacy.

I'll do my two routines, I'll be dynamite, my career will be under way, and I can kiss Peter goodbye and kiss Wayne hello.

Ten

"Hello everyone! We're back again, despite popular demand. It's the Peter Zero show, with my special guests, witty and wicked Joey Merino—say something wicked, Joey."

"Pride, avarice, lust, envy, gluttony, anger, and sloth."

"Isn't she a riot, folks? And our favorite Midnight Warbler, Dinah Smythe. Warble something for us, Dinah."

"Warble," Dinah said.

Peter did a double take. Dinah was a lot more relaxed than I expected, and her mild attempt at humor was the first funny thing I'd ever heard her say.

It better be the last. This show ain't big enough for two zanies.

Peter was oozing confidence. With Peter Zero turned on, there was no trace of the old Peter Stillman, the boy who was too shy to talk to anyone except me.

"Yes, we have an exciting couple of hours ahead. Let's start out with one of our exclusive WRTP Moldy Golden Oldies. Remember where you were the first time you heard this one? Top of the charts, 1921, Sophie Tucker's sensational hit, 'Lovin' Sam, the Sheik of Alabam'.'"

Peter checked the log. "You do Cockeyed Harry right after this," he told me. "Just go right into it." He turned to Dinah. "You're doing great, Dinah."

Great? She said one word.

"You're so cool tonight," he said.

She smiled warmly. "You showed me I could do it. Now I believe it. Because *you* believed in me."

"I do, I do," he said earnestly. "I believe in you."

"I believe I'm going to toss my supper," I remarked.

"Joey," Peter warned.

The record ended. My turn.

"And now a message from Cockeyed Harry's House of Audio," I read. "Folks, if it's AC, DC, AM or FM, if it's Beta or VHS, RCA or GE, you can get it at Cockeyed Harry's and you can get it cheap. I mean, we're talking cheap.

"Let's face it. This man's entire family is trying to have him declared incompetent so they can take over the business and start charging realistic prices for this stuff. Confidentially, he's not called Cockeyed Harry because he drives a hard bargain. Get the picture?

"Just walk into any of Cockeyed Harry's six Long Island locations and find out what a pushover this guy is. If you're the kind of person who likes to steal candy from a baby, you're going to love taking advantage of Cockeyed Harry.

"Cockeyed Harry's House of Audio—you'd be crazy to go anyplace else."

I sat back with a little smile and dropped the commercial on the floor. Peter grinned and shrugged, as if to say, "Okay, if that's what the sponsor wants."

We started a discussion on lying. I read an article in a magazine about why people tell lies. Peter liked the idea because he thought it would get people stirred up about morality and ethics and all that stuff. I liked it because it went well with one of the routines I planned to do.

"Sometimes a little fib spares someone's feelings," I said. "Like if your mother says to you, 'What did you get on your math test?' You know how upset she's going to be if you tell her you got a three. You don't want to put your mother through that agony. So you tell her the teacher is sick and you haven't gotten the tests back yet."

"But the teacher has to come back sometime," Peter said. "What do you tell your mother then?"

"Then *you* get sick," Dinah chimed in, "till your mother realizes how trivial grades are compared to your health."

I thought Peter was going to fall out of his chair—and onto Dinah. It must have taken all his restraint to keep from throwing his arms around her and crying, "What a trouper! What talent! What wit!"

100

I know it took all my restraint to keep from going for her throat.

Dinah looked delighted with herself. And surprised. Peter looked delighted with Dinah. And surprised. Meanwhile, nothing was going out over the airwaves, and up in his booth, Elroy was signaling one minute to news.

I jabbed Peter in the ribs. Just to get his attention. I might have jabbed him a little harder than I meant to. His "OUCH!" definitely carried over the air.

"Peter Zero is momentarily indisposed," I said smoothly, "but he'll be back with you after this update from WRTP's crack news team. And stay tuned for more laughs, your phone calls, and a special treat from me, Joey Merino, the dazzling new comedian you've all been hearing about."

The red ON THE AIR light went off.

Peter turned on me in fury. "This is my show! Stop trying to take over!"

"It's a dirty job," I said, "but somebody's got to do it. You were—um—preoccupied."

He rubbed his ribs.

"Does it hurt, Peter?" Dinah asked sympathetically.

"Ooh," I said, "did the big hundwed-and-ten pound bully hurt wittle Peter?"

Wittle Peter looked as if he were going to pitch the hundwed-and-ten pound bully through Elroy's glass window.

He clenched his fists in his lap till his knuckles turned white. "Just keep your hands to yourself

101

and stop trying to upstage me," he said threateningly.

"Good advice all around," I agreed. I shot Dinah a pointed stare.

Peter spent the rest of the news break rubbing his side and telling Dinah how great she'd been. "You just speak up whenever you feel like it," he cooed. "Don't be shy about joining in."

He stroked her arm and squeezed her hand. I toyed with the idea of getting an ice-cold Coke from the machine downstairs and pouring it in his lap.

"Let me get this straight," I said carefully. "She can talk whenever she feels like it, but I'm supposed to shut up unless I have your permission to speak. Is that what you're saying, *Mein Führer?*"

Peter sighed. "You never ask for my permission to talk."

"Joey, don't worry," Dinah said. "I'm not going to say that much. I don't want to replace you."

Peter gazed at her as if he were worshipping a goddess.

You already have. "Just don't do it on the air."

"Lighten up, will you?" Peter said. "You're acting like a spoiled brat. You're going on in one minute. Your 'fans' want you to be funny, and you sound like a shrew in training."

"Just don't try and tame me, Petruchio," I snapped. "You've got enough on your hands already."

But he was right. It was time to forget everything but Numero Uno. Peter wasn't important. Last week didn't count. The next few minutes could be crucial to my whole life. They could mean the difference be-

102

tween stardom and starvation, Comedy Queen or Burger King.

Elroy signaled us.

"We're back with the Peter Zero show and I want all you folks out there in Radioland to give a great, big hand to a brand new star in the comedy cosmos, Joey Merino. H-e-e-re's Joey!"

I took a deep breath.

Look out, World.

"Thank you, Peter. I know you listeners are expecting to hear a comedian, but tonight I want to talk to you about a very serious subject.

"Some of you are unemployed, and some of you have dull, dreary jobs that don't make the best use of your abilities. Tonight, as a public service, I want to tell you about Merino's Creative Résumé Writers, the sure-fire way to a top-flight job.

"You know, most people don't know anything about writing a résumé. The first mistake they make is that they tell the truth. Let me emphasize this point very strongly: Getting a good job has nothing to do with telling the truth.

"I hear what you're saying. 'Is Joey telling me to *lie?*' No. Not at all. I'm telling you to be creative. From years of experience writing résumés for people who now have exciting, high-class jobs, I know that the key to getting a super career is in your résumé.

"For instance. One of my clients worked on a garbage truck. He wanted to get a job in an art museum. He couldn't even get in for an interview. Why? Because he called himself a garbageman.

103

"When I prepared his résumé I wrote: 'For the last fifteen years I have been deeply involved in collecting. This pursuit has developed my sharp eye for weeding out treasures from trash, and I have saved numerous valuable artifacts from the junkheap.'

"Was that a lie? No. It was just a creative description of his job experience. He is now working in the acquisitions department of a major museum in the Southwest.

"'But, Joey,' you say, 'nobody can help me. I haven't worked in eleven years. I spend all my time watching soap operas.' Let me tell you something. If you've spent eleven years watching soaps, you're already qualified to be a doctor, a lawyer, a hired killer, or the head of a vast family fortune.

"You think it's hopeless? You think even I can't help you? One of my clients was in the clink for two years. Her dream was to be a flight attendant when she got sprung.

"I wrote that she had extensive experience in dealing with people from all walks of life, that she worked well in small spaces, that she looked good in a uniform.

"Friends, I helped these people and I can help you too. Why settle for a drab, low-paying job or no job at all? Merino's Creative Résumé Writers can get you into the fast lane faster than you can say 'Megabucks.'

"And what's the cost of this incredible, life-changing service? Ten dollars. You heard me right. Only ten dollars for a résumé that will lead you to the pot of gold at the end of the rainbow.

" 'But, Joey,' you ask me, 'how can you do that? How can you charge so little and give me so much?' I'm public-spirited, friends. I live to serve. I sincerely want to help people make better lives for themselves."

I paused for two seconds and prepared for the windup.

"Of course ... once you get that dream job, you won't want your boss to find out you're not qualified for it. *Nooo problem.* Merino's Career Training Schools will teach you all you need to keep your job in any one of thirty-nine high-paying careers, from architecture to zookeeping.

"That," I finished, "is where we make the *real* money."

"Joey Merino, folks!" Peter said. "Wasn't she *wonderful*?"

I didn't realize how nervous I was until the whole thing was over. Peter read a real commercial and I took long, deep breaths and tried to replay the routine in my mind.

How did it go over? How did I sound? This was the first chance my public had to hear me do a whole monologue, and I found that now, a minute later, I could hardly remember doing it.

I glanced at the phone board. Maybe someone would call in and tell me how hilarious I was. Maybe my future manager was, at this very moment...

But the lights were off. Peter didn't give out the phone number yet, I reminded myself. When he announces the number, that's when I'll hear from my fans.

"...Dinah Smythe, singing her way into your hearts ...take phone calls right after Dinah's song... the phone number is..."

Oh, sure. Give the number now, so everyone can call in and make a fuss over your no-talent tootsie.

Joey, I told myself, that's paranoid.

No, I replied, it's not paranoid.

His mouth slightly open, Peter watched Dinah sing. He couldn't take his eyes off her. When she finished the song she shot him a hopeful smile, as if to say, "That's the best I can do. Do you still love me?"

The answer was written all over Peter's dopey face.

Sure enough, all six phone lights were blinking now.

"Howdy."

"Hey!" Peter said, "it's our old pal Bronco Billy. I saw *Trouble on the Pecos* last week. Did you watch yourself?"

"Shore did."

It was *my* idea to watch the movie. I was the one who was supposed to tell Bronco Billy how much I liked it, even though I've never been a big Western fan. (Ever since Peter made me sit through *The Horse Soldiers* on TV, I get a rash at the sight of a saddlebag.)

But at least I got to see what Bronco Billy looked like—sort of a cross between David Hartman and Soupy Sales.

"I especially liked your singing," Dinah said.

"Thank you," he drawled. "I liked your singin' too."

"What about my knee-slappin' humor?" I cut in.

"Yeah," he grunted. "I got a few chuckles out of that."

"Whoo! Don't overdo the compliments or I'll start to get a swelled head." I was seething. That moth-eaten cowpuncher preferred Dinah's insipid twittering to my incisive social satire.

I was about to zap him back with a question about Bronco Billy's Rangeburgers, but he was already talking about *Trouble on the Pecos,* and the hilarious tricks the stuntmen played on him. Like putting glue on his saddle.

If gluing someone to a saddle is Bronco Billy's idea of knee-slappin' humor, I could hardly expect him to appreciate my material.

A very sensible attitude—but somehow not all that comforting.

Billy went on and on—and on. Peter even asked him to uke and yodel over the phone. I'd tuned out by this time. Every once in a while I yawned broadly, or dropped my head back and let my mouth hang open like I'd lapsed into a stupor.

Peter kept Billy on the phone for almost seven minutes. When they finally exchanged cowboy farewells ("Ride 'em easy"; "Happy trails"), I had my head pillowed on my arms in front of my mike, pretending to be fast asleep.

Elroy ran some taped commercials. Peter tapped me on the shoulder. "Wake up, Joey. We're going to take phone calls after this."

I "woke up" with a start. "Oh! Am I still here?"

It was 12:47. "How time flies when you're having fun."

"You did your routine only fifteen minutes ago," Peter pointed out.

"Yeah, but what have you done for me lately?"

"You'll get to talk enough. Look at those phones."

"Oh, sure. Everyone's forgotten I'm here by now. What with Bronco Billy and the silver-tongued thrush."

"There's no need to be sarcastic," Dinah said. She sounded like a teacher reprimanding a third grader.

"Put on your headphones," Peter ordered. I'd taken them off so I could "sleep" more comfortably.

"Yes, master." Joke it up, Joey. Just get through the next hour and ten minutes, do one more boffo routine, and walk out of this studio—and Peter's life—forever.

I hardly needed my headphones. Most of the calls were about Bronco Billy. Dinah got two fan calls and two people called to say I was funny.

One was my brother Andy.

By the time we cut to the news, I was ready to walk out of the studio—and Peter's life—right then and there. No matter how I tried to tell myself there was only one more hour to go, I began to wonder if I could make it through one more minute.

I was being ignored. It wasn't just having to share the spotlight with someone else. I couldn't even get on the stage. It was humiliating. For all anyone knew, I could have passed out at the mike and been carried off on a stretcher.

And no one cared. Including Peter. Especially Peter.

I yanked off my headphones.

"Why did you say we'd take more phone calls after the news?" I demanded. "We're supposed to talk about TV commercials to start the second hour."

"I know," Peter said, "but I want to stay with the phones for a while. We've really got them interested out there."

"Interested?" I said angrily. "How could they be interested in half an hour of tumbling tumbleweeds and prairie-dog flop?"

"That's what the listeners want," Peter said. "Look at the phone lines. Just because you don't like Westerns doesn't mean—"

"Look, Peter, how about letting me do my routine before you take the calls? Right after the news." At least that way someone might remember I was supposed to be the main zany around here. At least my show biz angel might not fall asleep, stupefied by another forty minutes of stale sagebrush nostalgia.

"No way. You helped make up the program log. You know what the schedule is. You do your routine at one-forty."

"But you're changing the schedule anyway!"

"I can do that, Joey," he said. "It's my show."

If he said *my* show one more time—

"I haven't been on any more than you have," Dinah remarked, "and you don't hear me complaining."

"You're a saint," I muttered. "An absolute saint."

"*Really.*" She sounded positively patronizing.

"Let's remember," Peter said, "that we're all happy

members of the Peter Zero radio family. So when we get back on the air we won't sound like we need a social worker to moderate the program."

"One of us family members isn't happy!" I yelled. "One of us is sitting here like a dead houseplant and one of us is sick of it!"

"Joey," Peter said wearily, "put a cork in it. And don't take it out until we're back on the air, which is in one minute. You'll speak to the callers, you'll do your routine, and we'll talk about why you don't work and play well with others later."

I put a cork in it. I was too flabbergasted to do anything else. I didn't know this person. Talk about Jekyll and Hyde! Best friends for almost five years, and I didn't know him. Give him a microphone and Princess Di and he turns into an arrogant, domineering petty tyrant.

Self-confidence is fine, but carried too far it can become megalomania. If Peter developed his budding Napoleonic complex much further, he'd end up listening to RTP in the Home for the Incurably Silly.

I wasn't in much of a mood for bantering with the callers after that, even though three people actually phoned in to ask when I'd be on again.

"Stay tuned," Peter told them. "You'll hear Joey Merino again right after the one-thirty news. We're saving her for the big finish."

If that was his attempt to soothe my feelings, it didn't work. At any other time I might have appreciated the buildup, but not right after he'd shot me down. My feelings were not sootheable.

I psyched myself up for five minutes before I did my routine at one-forty—exactly on schedule. While I was on, I found I could concentrate only on my delivery, as if Peter and Dinah weren't there. I was getting pretty good at turning negative emotions into positive energy.

I did my bit about how all these self-help books taught me how to lose friends and bore people, and led me from riches to rags in a few short weeks.

I thought I put it over really well, but I felt more relief than anything else when I finished. I'd done what I'd set out to do, and if no show biz biggies called, well, maybe my expectations had been a little unrealistic. At least I'd gotten a chance to be heard, a chance to reach a potential fifty thousand people. Maybe my name wasn't a household word yet, but I was still better known than I had been two weeks ago.

And I'd never walk into this studio again. The maiden aunt of the Peter Zero family is checking out.

As for Peter Stillman....

Talk about unrealistic expectations.

Eleven

I walked to school Monday and Tuesday. Peter had called several times on Sunday, but I hung up on him. He was Numero Uno on my list of people I would never speak to again.

When Andy answered the phone and told me Peter said it was important, I said, "Tell him to put a cork in it."

It was only eight blocks to school, and the sun was shining both days, so I could afford to be independent until I was able to scrounge a ride from someone else.

When I got to school on Tuesday I spotted a small crowd milling around in the parking lot. I walked over to see what was happening.

"There's Joey!" somebody yelled. "Hey, Joey, come here. You're in the paper!"

"What?"

April Abruzzo grabbed my arm and pulled me into

the center of the crowd. The center of the crowd con-
sisted of Peter and Dinah. They were each holding a
copy of *Newsday*, "Long Island's Largest Daily Newspaper."

"Show Joey," April urged. "Dinah, show Joey."

"Here." Dinah held out the page for me to see. Three
kids leaned over my shoulder and read the headline out
loud with me:

"'BRONCO BILLY BELL BACK IN THE SADDLE
AGAIN: LAST OF THE SINGING COWBOYS REDISCOVERED ON
LOCAL RADIO SHOW.'"

"Where am *I*?" I asked. "This is all about Bronco
Billy."

"Keep reading," Dinah said. "You'll get to it."

My small chorus chanted along with me: "'Bronco
Billy Bell, a former cowboy star in the late forties and
early fifties, is suddenly finding his dormant career re-
vitalized because of a phone call he made to a local
radio station in the wee hours of the morning.

"'The WRTP program, a fill-in for regular Dakota
Stone, features three students from James P. Jefferson
High School—'"

"YAY!" yelled the chorus.

"See?" said April. "There you are."

"'—Peter Stillman, Joey Marino, and Dinah Smyth.'"

"*Ma*rino!" I wailed. "They spelled my name wrong."

"They spelled my name wrong too," Dinah pointed
out calmly.

"Don't start being a saint again," I warned her. I
glared at Peter. "When did all this happen?"

"A reporter came over on Sunday to interview me."

113

"Why didn't you tell me?"

He shrugged. "I tried to."

That's why he'd kept calling Sunday. And I'd kept hanging up on him. Boy, did I blow it. What a day I picked to start never speaking to Peter again.

"You could have been a little more insistent," I said. "Considering that you knew how important this would be to me."

"I told Andy it was important. He told me to put a cork in it. After that I figured the lines of communication were pretty much shut down."

"They shut down two weeks ago," I snapped. "Didn't you notice?"

Three kids moved closer to us, listening to our little discussion more eagerly than to Dinah's reading.

Suddenly an elusive idea that had nagged me for days became as clear as if it were spelled out in capital letters. Communication between Peter and me had really been closed for *years*, not weeks. I didn't have a chance to absorb this revelation then. I had to hear the rest of the article.

"'... call to his old agent, Swifty Carew, who came out to catch the show with Bronco Billy ... visiting his daughter on Long Island ... tremendous listener response....'"

I didn't want to act temperamental in front of my fans, but so far the Main Zany of the show, good old Joey Merino, had been mentioned only once—as a misprint.

"This is all about Bronco Billy," I said. "Skip to the part where they talk about us. You *did* talk to the reporter about the rest of us, didn't you?" I asked Peter.

"Yes, I talked to the reporter about the rest of us," Peter said. "And I spelled your name for him three times."

"I just speed-read the whole article," Gary Wade announced. "There isn't any part about you guys."

"BOO!" the kids chorused.

"I think that's just terrible." April wedged herself between Peter and me. "After all, it's *your* show, Peter. You're the star. Bronco Billy would be nowhere if it wasn't for *you.*"

I almost laughed, in spite of that rotten story. If April Abruzzo was going to hit on Peter, Dinah would have her hands full.

Of course, so would Peter.

He'll manage, I thought bitterly. Look how good he's getting dealing with crowds.

Gary Wade wedged himself between April and Peter. The lust in his heart was plain as he eyed April. "April's right," he said. "No matter what *Newsday* thinks, you guys are the only reason we listen to the show."

"Yeah! Right! Right on!"

"Thanks for the vote of confidence, friends," Peter said. "But what are you going to do? That's show biz."

"I know what I'm going to do," I said. I grabbed the article out of his hands and ripped the page into tiny little shreds.

The audience went wild.

Peter was standing in front of my locker at three o'clock.

115

"I want to talk to you," he said gravely.

"Well, *I* don't want—" I stopped myself. I remembered the stray thought that had flitted through my mind this morning. I remembered how I cursed myself for being so stubborn about talking to Peter on the phone Sunday.

"What do you want to talk about?" I pulled some books from my locker. I'd have plenty of time to study this week.

"You," he said. "Me."

"And 'It'?"

"You mean the show?" he asked.

"No, I mean Tweety Pie." I slammed my locker door shut. "Well?"

He frowned. "Yeah. Dinah too."

"Oh goody. Sounds like a divine afternoon."

We didn't say anything in the car, which made me wonder if this attempt to talk about "Us"—and "It"— was going to give us any more insight into each other than the last four and a half years had.

Because that's what I'd realized in the parking lot. Even though we'd hung out together since eighth grade, I really didn't know very much about Peter, except for superficial things. And he knew even less about me.

What made me think that just because you spend a lot of time with a person, you really know him?

I mean, sure, I could tell when he was down, but I hardly ever knew why. If I asked he'd deny it, or say it was no big deal. Most of the time I didn't push him

116

any further. I just crossed my eyes or did my Donald Duck imitation until he laughed.

I knew he was shy with girls, but I didn't know if he wanted not to be. I was sure he never had romantic fantasies about me, but I didn't know if he had romantic fantasies at all.

I could understand that this was a topic he might feel squeamish about discussing with me—but then what *have* we been talking about all this time?

WRTP. Rock groups. Math tests. School gossip. His uncle. My brothers. Comedians. Christmas shopping.

Did he ever cry? Did he ever sit at his window and wish that his father would come walking down the street? Did he resent his mother for working and leaving him with housekeepers till he was eleven?

Did he have dreams of being a hero and adventuring in exotic lands, or did he just want to take a tour of Motown?

How did he feel when I kissed him in the kitchen?

If anyone asked him the same kinds of questions about me, he wouldn't know the answers either. *He never wanted to know,* I realized. I've spent almost a third of my life with a person who never wanted to find out if there was anybody inside my clown suit except a clown.

We sat at opposite ends of Peter's living room couch. If we were any farther apart we'd be in different time zones. I wished I hadn't agreed to this talk. I felt like a volcano, ready to erupt under the slightest pressure.

This "friend" had treated me like a child, an enemy, a houseplant, on his show—when he remembered I was there. This "friend" could have found a way to get through to me on Sunday if he really wanted to.

Like, for instance, telling Andy that there was a reporter at his house and if I wanted some publicity to come right over.

This "friend" might restrain himself from slobbering over his no-talent tootsie in my presence.

I should have stuck to my resolution never to speak to him again. It was years too late for talk, and it would take months to yank out all the slings and arrows he'd hurled at me.

"Joey," he began tentatively, "Dinah asked me to—"

"*Dinah?* What happened to you and me?"

"That's what I want to know. You've changed. Ever since we started doing the show you've been so touchy I never know when you're going to dump on me. And when you dump, you *dump.*"

"It is not perfectly clear," I said, "which one of us is the dumper and which is the dumpee."

He shook his head. "I don't know what you're talking about. You're the one who refused to talk to me for three days."

"But *you* haven't changed," I said. "You're still the nice, simple, unspoiled guy you always were. You're not stomping on people with lead boots as you climb the ladder of success, right?"

"Hey, give me a break. I already apologized for cutting off your routine on the first show. But I had to. I have to run the program. That's my *job.*"

"Don't tell me, don't tell me. It's *your* show."

"Well, it is," he said. "And if anybody's stomping on people, it's you. You clawed me last week, you punched me Saturday... you're getting so *physical.*"

"Yeah, that really scares you, doesn't it?" I muttered.

"What is your *problem!*" he demanded. "I know you're mad at me, even if I don't know why, but do you have to take it out on Dinah? You're treating her like a piece of—"

"So we are talking about Dinah!" I yelled. I jumped up from the couch. "If Dinah wasn't upset we wouldn't be here pretending to talk about you and me. Well, you can tell Dinah she won't have Joey Merino to kick her around anymore. And you won't have to strain your limited resources to try and 'communicate' with me again."

"Does that mean you're not going to be on my last show?"

I went up like Mt. Saint Helens. "Dinah and your show!" I screamed. "That's what you really wanted to talk about!"

I grabbed a throw pillow from the couch and charged him.

"You hypocrite!" I pounded him on the head and face with the pillow. "You arrogant, swell-headed, blind, unfeeling—"

"Jesus, Joey!" He held his arms over his head to protect himself. "Stop it! What's wrong with you?"

119

He got hold of the pillow and yanked it away from me. He grabbed my wrists and held on. "Cut it out, or I'm going to forget I'm not allowed to hit girls."

I started to cry.

He pulled me down on the couch next to him. "What is going *on* here? I never saw you like this."

"You never saw me, period. Forget it. It doesn't matter now."

"Yes, it does. Why are you crying? Why did you hit me?"

I sat there, trying to catch my breath, trying to stop crying. I wiped my eyes. "Everything's changed," I said finally. "You've changed. You really did turn into Peter Zero."

"You don't like that," he said.

"I don't like being treated—oh, what's the difference whether I like the new you or not?" I got up to get my purse. I pulled out a bunch of tissues. I must look a mess, I thought. But that *certainly* didn't matter anymore.

"Are you kidding?" Peter said. "Hey, we've been friends too long—"

"That's just the point," I cut in. "We've been *friends* too long."

"You're still not getting through to me—"

"I never did!" I whirled around to face him. "Not even when I kissed you smack in the middle of your kitchen! That was too subtle for you? My meaning was unclear? I'm sorry. I didn't think you'd need a translator."

He looked dazed. He stared at me in disbelief for a moment, then looked away.

"This is really embarrassing," he mumbled.

"*Tell* me about it."

"I thought it was a joke," he said slowly. "I mean, a bit, you know. You're always kidding around..."

"That's me all right. A laugh a minute. Good old Joey."

"But that *is* you." He got up from the couch and moved toward me. "At least, it used to be. I mean, I thought you were. I never realized...listen, that was a very jokey kiss."

"*Not to me it wasn't.*" Oh, God, I thought, I can't stand this. The only response he felt when I kissed him was the urge to laugh?

"Peter, please take me home now. I don't want to talk anymore. I'm feeling really stupid."

I couldn't figure out the expression on his face as he handed me my jacket.

"*You* feel stupid?" he said. "How do you think *I* feel?"

Twelve

"Hello, Joey. Charlie Bliss here. How's my new star?"

"Hi, Mr. Bliss. I'm okay. My twinkle isn't exactly lighting up the solar system, but other than that—"

Other than that everything stinks. And I'm not okay.

"You'd be surprised," he said. "Listener reaction has been very favorable."

I kicked the door of my room shut. Andy was torturing his keyboard and Matt was playing Van Halen on the stereo. My parents weren't home from work yet or it would have been a lot quieter in the house.

"Did anybody mention me by name?" I asked.

"A lot of people," he said vaguely. "Most of them wanted to hear more of you." He paused for a moment. "I told Peter that."

"What did he say?" I tried not to sound suspicious, but I thought Uncle Charlie was laying it on a little

122

thick. I wanted to believe that people were clamoring to hear me, but I wondered if that was the only reason for this call.

"He said you probably wouldn't do the show at all. I don't understand why. Our rating for the second show was three-tenths of a point higher than Dakota Stone ever got."

"That much?" I tried to sound impressed.

"It may not sound like a lot to you, but if it goes up a half point we get to charge the advertisers more money. And we've got a good shot at that this week, after the publicity in *Newsday*."

Yes, let's not forget the publicity in *Newsday*.

"It's really nice that you're so interested in me, Mr. Bliss, but to tell you the truth, I don't know why you are. I mean, all those people will listen whether I'm on the show or not. Bronco Billy got all the headlines. Who cares about Joey *Marino*?"

"Don't you realize how many show business people are going to be listening to the show because of him? And if Peter schedules this right, they're going to hear a whole lot of Joey Merino before Bronco Billy gets his five minutes."

What a temptation. I was so angry about that newspaper article and the way Peter threw away my chance to meet the press that I never considered what Bronco Billy's publicity could mean to me.

Who had heard me on the first two shows? The WRTP faithful—those two Cub Scouts, the pregnant ladies, and the silly people. They couldn't do anything for me careerwise. But all the agents and producers I kept hoping to hear from would actually be out there listening this time.

And if Peter scheduled it right—

What a joke. Peter couldn't schedule anything right. Not in Radioland, not in real life.

And how in the world could I face him again after what happened Tuesday? Forget it, comedy fans.

"You should think of your own best interests," he went on. "Another thing—Harry Taubman wants you to have lunch with him on Monday."

My first thought was, Oh, good. I won't have to eat the fish sticks. My second thought was, Who's Harry Taubman?

"He hinted that he has big plans for you," Mr. Bliss said tantalizingly.

"Ohh, Cockeyed Harry. What big plans?" I was intrigued. I couldn't begin to imagine what Cockeyed Harry had in mind, unless he wanted to hire me as a copywriter; I wasn't ready to give up stardom to write Cockeyed Harry commercials.

"He wants to meet you before he says anything definite."

I was lost by this time.

"Look," I said, "I'm very grateful for the chance you gave me, but I'm not that vital to your station for you to spend all this time trying to persuade me to do just one little show. You may never hear me say that again," I added.

"All right. I'll be perfectly frank. I really am interested in your welfare, but I don't think you're that important to the station either."

"You didn't have to agree with me so fast," I said.

"But Harry Taubman's advertising money is. And *he* thinks you're important. He's got a real bee in his bonnet about you, and Harry can be pretty unpleasant when he doesn't get what he wants. Harry wants you, and I need Harry's commercials. There you have it."

"Thanks for being honest. I guess. It's nice *somebody* wants me, but—"

"I hate to pull this on you, Joey, but if you feel any—um—gratitude toward me, now's the time to show it."

Aw, Uncle Charlie, don't do this to me.

"I'll have to think about it," I said dully. "There are other factors involved."

"It's Thursday. You haven't much time to decide. Look, whatever's going on between you and Peter, don't you think it would be a good idea to settle it and get back to normal again?"

There was no getting back to normal, I thought, as we said goodbye. I didn't even know what normal was. But I recognized a point of no return when I saw one.

I thought it was all "settled" Saturday night, as soon as my last routine was over. Then I thought we'd "settled" it Tuesday afternoon, by talking openly, at last, about our feelings. But opening up had left me feeling like a fool, and Peter—who knows? I hadn't been able to speak to him since.

We had history together, but fortunately, April Abruzzo kept him so occupied with her sudden consuming interest in radio that while we waited for the class to start we could pretend we didn't see each other.

And now what? Do we pretend not to see each other for the rest of the year? And what about next year? Do I ignore him forever?

What had we settled? Peter knew how I felt about him, and I knew how he felt about Dinah, but we didn't seem to be able to handle how we felt about each other.

Maybe it was too soon for me to get over everything that had happened, but if I had some real sense of conclusion, if I found a decent way to write "The End" on the last four and a half years and two weeks, maybe I could get past the point of no return and go forward with the rest of my life.

Now Mr. Bliss was calling in his IOUs. I was too distracted and depressed to wonder what Cockeyed Harry had planned for me. I didn't even care that much. Whatever it was, I was sure it wasn't what *I* had planned for me.

But I knew what Charlie Bliss had done, and when he pushed that Guilt button, I really did feel like a stubborn, spiteful ingrate.

I *owed* him one more show. Nothing he said, from the promise of producers listening to the lure of lunch with the Emperor of Electronics, could have persuaded me to do another show. I couldn't imagine a more miserable situation than trying to be funny while locked in with the two people in the world who made me feel the worst about myself.

No, nothing could tempt me to go through that

again—except knowing that I might feel even more rotten if I refused Mr. Bliss this one favor.

Perhaps that was the last logical thought I had that afternoon. Maybe my brain circuits were overloaded by all the decisions and all my warring emotions, but suddenly the solution was very clear.

What I had to do to bring this period of my life to a graceful conclusion was to talk to Dinah.

It was the only way, since if I killed her I'd get ten years to life. I would go to her and apologize for the way I acted. I'm a big enough person to admit my mistakes. I would give up all claim to Peter's affections (what choice did I have anyway?), give the two of them my blessing, and be at peace with myself and the world.

Then I'd be able to let go of my jealousy and resentment, we could do the last show like civilized professionals, Uncle Charlie would be happy, and I'd end up smelling like a rose.

I might droop and shed a few petals for a while; it's hard to give up a fantasy when you've held on to it for so long. But you can't expect your head to stop hurting if you keep banging it against a brick wall.

I felt positively noble as I picked up the phone to call Dinah.

Thirteen

I didn't blame Dinah for sounding suspicious when I asked to come over and talk to her. Since the first night she climbed into Peter's car with her guitar, I hadn't said anything to her that could possibly be construed as friendly.

But my aura of serenity, my inner glow at the grand gesture of self-sacrifice I was about to make, my burning determination to make peace with everybody and myself, lighted the way up the stairs to Dinah's room.

At least that's how I pictured it.

Saint Joey the Peacemaker, I thought. I glanced around Dinah's elegant cream and peach room.

"Well? What did you want to talk about?" Dinah asked. "I'm pretty busy." She turned off the little TV next to her bed.

I hadn't planned what to say. I just raced over to Dinah's in Matt's car a minute after I called her. I'm a good improviser. I figured I'd think it up as I went along. I'd always managed before.

"I never pictured you watching TV," I said. I meant it as a compliment.

"Why should you picture me at all?"

Not the greatest of starts, but I knew how to work up to a boffo finish. For an instant I flashed on Peter's face when Dinah told him about this. I could see the tears in his eyes as he realized how truly admirable I was.

"Dinah," I began again, "let's be honest. I know that relations between us have been a little—um—strained."

"How well you put it. I would have said we hate each other's guts."

"Yes, well, that's certainly getting off to a nice, honest start."

She sat cross-legged on her peach bedspread. I had the feeling she would not care to have me sit next to her on her peach bedspread, so I turned her desk chair around and sat facing the bed.

"Some of the things I said to you were kind of nasty," I admitted, "but—"

"All the things you said to me were nasty."

"But there were forces at work," I persisted, "that you couldn't have known about. It wasn't fair to—"

She laughed. "You mean that you were jealous because Peter liked me?"

"How did you know that?"

"An idiot would have known that," she snapped.

"Peter didn't."

She shrugged. "Peter's a little immature."

"*Immature!*" How dare she talk about Peter that way! Behind his back. In front of my face. Maybe he'd had a sluggish puberty, but he wasn't immature.

This is not working out the way I planned, I thought. What's going wrong? Maybe I'm not being humble enough? Maybe I ought to forget the buildup and go straight to the boffo finish.

"All right, okay, Dinah, just listen a minute. I was jealous and I said crummy things to you because of that and I've come to apologize. It wasn't personal—I would have been just as mean to anyone who went after Peter—"

"*Went after Peter!*" she said threateningly. She uncrossed her legs and moved toward the edge of the bed. I noticed she had a whole lot of dangerous throw pillows on the spread.

"Bad choice of words," I said. "Dinah, I'm apologizing. Listen to me. I'm humbling myself in front of you, begging for forgiveness because I know I was rotten to you. I don't get any humbler than this, so don't louse it up, will you? Just tell me you forgive me, for Pete's sake—for *Peter's* sake. For the sake of the show. Even if you still hate me."

"Now *you* listen, funny girl," Dinah said. "I don't need you, or your apology or your friendship."

"That last possibility was pretty remote anyway."

"You can outtalk me and out-insult me six days of the week, but today is the seventh day and you're going to rest your mouth for a little while."

I nearly fell off the chair. If this girl really put her

mind to it, she might be able to outtalk me *three* days of the week.

"All I wanted," Dinah said, "was to see if I could do it. *That's all.* You didn't know I wrote songs, did you?"

I shook my head.

"You didn't know anything about me, did you?"

"I know you're good at everything," I replied. "Actually, I always sort of thought of you as Ms. Perfect."

"What a crock! You still don't know anything about me."

This sounded awfully familiar for some reason.

"Nobody knows anything about me," she went on. "All they see is what you see. Surface—that's all. Whatever you think of my songs or my singing, that was the only time I let a little of *me* show. A part of me nobody ever saw before."

This was *weird.* Not just that Dinah was opening up to me, but what she was saying.

"But everybody thought you were good," I said, "so what are you angry about?"

"You don't think so. Not that I care about your opinion."

I suspected that she really did care, though I couldn't imagine why. I had a funny feeling I'd thought this before too, sometime.

"I was prejudiced," I said. "It really wasn't personal. If you were a juggler I'd have made snide juggler jokes."

Her lips twitched a little, like she might laugh. But she held it in. I guess she'd gotten pretty good at that.

Welcome to the club, honey.

"I did *not* go after Peter. I only asked him to let me

131

be on the show once. It was a test. When nobody laughed at me, and when I didn't make a complete ass of myself, I thought maybe letting people see me a little differently wasn't so dangerous."

"You passed the test," I said. "They loved you." Why was I trying to convince her? Go figure.

She shook her head impatiently. "That wasn't the test. It's like Samuel Johnson said about the dancing dog. The wonder of it wasn't that he was good, it was that he could do it at all."

"You lost me. Right around Samuel Johnson and the dog."

"Never mind. The thing was, all those people suddenly wanting to talk to me, being so friendly and encouraging—it felt good. I felt like they liked me."

"I know what you mean." I remembered all the phone calls, the kids flocking around us in the cafeteria after the first show.

"I was glad Peter gave me the chance to have that experience," she said. "But I never—" She seemed to close up again. "I don't know why I'm telling you all this."

Probably because I'd extended the hand of friendship and disarmed her with my noble gesture of sisterhood. Wait till I spring my next noble gesture. Wait till she hears how I'm giving up Peter for the sake of their happiness.

I stood up from the chair. "Just one more thing, Dinah. I won't stand in your way anymore. You can have Peter."

The Ice Princess nearly went up in flames. "*I don't*

132

want Peter. You can have him, with my blessings."

"*What!*" That's supposed to be my line. *I'm* supposed to give the blessings. I couldn't believe my ears. What about all those loving glances, the handholding, the intimate whispers, the mutual drooling?

And how could anyone not want Peter?

"What's wrong with Peter?" I demanded.

"Nothing," Dinah said. "I'm just not interested."

"But he's interested in you." What am I *saying!* Why am I playing matchmaker here when inside I should be going "Oooh! Oooh!" and outside I should be zipping off to go help Peter recover from his broken heart. Even if I wasn't speaking to him.

"I can't help that," she said. "I tried to—I mean, he did something really good for me and I felt grateful. But it didn't work out. I just don't like him that way. So take him. He's yours."

I was staggered. She sounded so cold, so indifferent. Didn't she know she was going to break Peter's heart? Not to mention undermining all of the confidence he'd gained from Peter Zero.

"I don't think," I said slowly, "that this is going to improve relations in the Peter Zero radio family."

"Don't you understand? There is no radio family. I'm not doing the show anymore. I didn't even want to do the second one. You can have Peter and you can have the show. That's what you both wanted all along. The only things he ever talked about were you and that stupid program."

"Really?" I breathed.

"Oh, grow up." She walked over to the TV and

133

snapped it on. "You two belong together. And you're the only people dim enough not to know it."

I zoomed down the stairs like I had wings on my boots. My feet may have never touched a step. I was out of the house, into Matt's car and halfway to the Stillmans' before my head cleared. Dinah might not have told Peter any of this yet.

If she hadn't, he'd probably be a tad upset if I burst into his house and announced, "I know Dinah doesn't love you but you still have me, even though you don't really want me, but I'll wait till you see what a blind fool you've been."

I made a screeching Y-turn and headed home.

Nothing is settled, I told myself. I'd apologized to Dinah, but I hadn't brought a tidy conclusion to this period of my life. Because this period of my life wasn't concluded yet.

I felt terrific as I pulled into the driveway.

I ought to make these noble gestures more often.

I debated whether or not to call Peter that evening. If he'd just found out that Dinah didn't love him he might not feel like talking. In fact, he might even think it was my fault that things didn't work out between them. Dinah had practically said so.

I thought how strange it was that she knew more about what Peter felt than I did, when she'd known him for only a couple of weeks. I knew now that you could be with a person for years and still not understand

134

him, but you'd think that I'd have picked up some vibrations if he ever sent any my way. I was certainly always looking for them.

But she said he didn't know we belonged together either. Maybe she was just smarter and more perceptive than us. Maybe she was more mature than we were. If she had a boyfriend in Yale or Harvard or Columbia, maybe she was more experienced.

And maybe, I thought, she's wrong.

At least I ought to tell Peter I'd do the show Saturday. I mean, he was probably afraid to ask me, considering I'd attacked him with a throw pillow the last time he mentioned it.

Call Uncle Charlie! What an inspiration. I'd relieve his mind and show my gratitude and he'd tell Peter. Then Peter would call me because the show was only two days away, and we'd have to start work fast.

I called Mr. Bliss and told him the news. Then I waited for Peter to call.

He didn't call.

I waited till eleven for the phone to ring before I gave up. He could be with Dinah right now, having his heart broken. Or maybe he saw her yesterday, or this afternoon. While I sit here at the phone, he might be curled up on his bed in a fetal position, clutching a pillow to his aching heart.

He probably wasn't thinking of me at all. For once, he might not even be thinking about his show.

I kept going over Dinah's words in my mind. If she was right, and he didn't know that we belonged together, he might try to get over his unhappy love affair by letting April Abruzzo soothe his wounded ego. What a horrible thought.

No, April wasn't his type.

How do I know what his "type" is? I don't know anything about him, except superficial things like—

"You didn't know anything about me, did you?" Dinah had said. "Surface—that's all you see."

No wonder I had that feeling of déjà vu!

This is all very bizarre, I thought, as I climbed into bed. I don't seem to know anything about anybody— although I learned more about Dinah than I ever wanted to know.

And nobody knows anything about me. Except Dinah.

But I *did* try. I told Peter that I wanted to be more than friends, and I ended up feeling humiliated.

What had Dinah said about going public with her songs? Something about opening herself up, testing to see if she could do it. And when no one laughed at her, she decided that letting a secret part of herself show wasn't so dangerous.

Peter didn't laugh at me when I opened up to him. He didn't think I was stupid. He thought *he* was stupid. Okay, so I was embarrassed and hurt. So I didn't score as high on my test as Dinah did.

Or did I? The important thing was that I'd tried. I hadn't acted like an ass—if you leave out the part with the throw pillows. I'd just surprised him.

Why should I expect anyone to know me? When the going gets tough, I go for the laughs. If Peter didn't know the "real me," was it because he didn't want to? Or because I wouldn't let him see?

Go for the laughs. Since I was twelve, those had been words to live by.

Bad choice of words?

Fourteen

I heard a horn honking outside our house next morning.

"Hey, Oscar," Andy called, "it's Felix."

It took me a minute to figure out what he meant. When I did, I grabbed him and hugged him. "Dear brother." I ruffled his hair. "Peter and I aren't such an odd couple, are we?"

"One of you is. Hey, don't mess up my hair. I just put mousse on it."

"How quickly they grow up," I said fondly. "It seems only yesterday you were dropping Jell-O down my jeans."

"Keep this up and I might do it again," Andy muttered.

The horn honked twice. I grabbed my coat and books and purse. "Do not ask for whom the horn honks!" I called out. "It honks for me. 'Bye all."

Andy was grumbling under his breath as I closed the door behind me.

I ran to Peter's car, flung the door open and hurled my books into the back seat. "Sir Galahad!" I cried. "Here to save me from the elements. Chivalry is not dead. Just resting." I slid into the seat beside him and shot him a great big friendly smile. He didn't smile back.

"What elements? It's almost fifty degrees and the sun is shining."

He shifted into reverse as I shifted into Good Old Joey. Cheer him up was my first instinct. Later, when he recovers from Dinah, is the time to get serious.

"The weather report said it's going to snow Sunday. I figured you're just a little early."

"How come you're such a bundle of joy this morning?" he asked.

"I'm thinking how happy you're going to be when I tell you I'll do the show with you tomorrow night."

He didn't look happy.

"Yeah. Uncle Charlie told me. I'm glad."

"I'm glad you're glad. Of course, I'd be gladder if you sounded a little gladder."

He didn't tell me to fasten my seat belt! He just started driving, without the "buckle-up-for-safety" bit. Maybe I ought to shut up and let him brood. He must have talked to Dinah. He must still be in shock.

"We'd better get together this afternoon," he said. "We haven't got much time to plan the program."

"It shouldn't be that hard. Aren't we going to do the same thing we've been doing?"

"Almost."

I ate lunch with Peter. Alone. He didn't say much. His eyes shifted around the lunchroom from time to time. I knew who he was looking for.

"Did you know that Cockeyed Harry is taking me to lunch Monday?" I asked. Anything to distract him. Anything to get him to stop looking around for Dinah.

"Yeah. Are you going to go?"

"It was a tough decision, what with having to miss the fish sticks, but I'll go. I wish I knew what it was about."

"I know what it is," Peter said. "I found out last night. He wants to check you out for TV commercials."

I choked on a piece of pizzaburger. "Do you know the Heimlich maneuver?" I gasped between coughs.

"If you can ask for it, you don't need it."

I managed to swallow the pizzaburger bit. "Look at this," I muttered. "He won't even put his arms around me when I'm dying."

"What?"

"Listen, what TV commercials? He's got a guy who does all of them already. Besides, I don't want to do commercials."

"You should have thought of that before you stole the first one."

"This is insane!" I cried.

Peter finally smiled. "They don't call him Cockeyed Harry for nothing."

140

"Peter, stop it. This is no time for jokes. I'm a comedian."

"There's a news flash for you."

"Would you get serious for a minute? You know, there's a time to be funny—"

He started to laugh.

"You're really enjoying this aren't you?" I said bitterly.

He nodded. "I'm having a pretty good time with it."

This was ridiculous. Even in the midst of my shock about Cockeyed Harry's plans, I recognized that Felix and Oscar were playing role reversal.

And Peter *was* having a good time. He was grinning broadly, his eyes were on my eyes and nowhere else... until he suddenly looked up and his eyes darkened.

"Hi, sugar." *Wayne.* I'd forgotten all about Wayne.

"I was looking all over for you," he said reproachfully. He slid onto the bench next to me. He put his arm around my shoulder. I felt a preliminary tingle. He squeezed my arm.

"So what are we going to do tomorrow night? We never decided. You want to go to the Kung Fu movie or bowling?"

His hand moved between my shoulder blades. He rubbed. Preliminary tingle turned to major tingle.

"Gee, Wayne, what a tough decision. But the thing is, I can't go out with you tomorrow. I have to do the show again."

"Aw, Joey, why do you keep putting me off like this?"

On the other side of me, Peter was very quiet. He wasn't even chewing.

I reached back and plucked Wayne's hand off my shoulder. I could think clearer that way. Without the distraction of involuntary biological reactions, it was easier to remember how boring Wayne was. I mean, do you want to go to a Kung Fu movie or bowling? That's like asking if I'd rather break my right leg or my left leg.

Merely because a person makes your toes curl and your pulse race faster than a speeding bullet, this does not make up for the long stretches of tedium you have to suffer between episodes of toecurling and pulse racing.

I don't want Wayne, I decided. Wayne is only good at one thing, and I need intellectual stimulation too. Behind his pretty face snoozed a lazy brain, rousing itself only when Wayne plotted makeout maneuvers.

"Wayne," I said softly, "I've been thinking about you a lot this week."

"Are you thinking what I'm thinking?" He leered.

"What I think is that we're not really right for each other. We don't have anything in common—"

I was trying to be kind, to let him down gently. After all, he'd been looking forward to me for two weeks, and I could imagine how disappointed he'd be when he found out I didn't want to see him anymore.

"Opposites attract. And we've got the most important thing in common, anyway." He cocked his head suggestively and raised one eyebrow.

Peter stood up. I thought he was going to leave the table, but instead he walked around the bench and sat himself down next to Wayne.

"Hey, Pete, how about a little privacy?" Wayne said.

"I just wanted to get a close-up look at Wayne Newberger striking out," Peter said. Actually, Peter Zero must have said it. Peter Stillman never would have. "This is a historic first, isn't it, big fella?"

"Now listen, *friend*—"

They're going to fight over me! I thought. I can't believe it. Two boys are going to fight over me. And one of them is Peter! I wanted to leap up on the table and belt out a few bars of the Hallelujah Chorus.

"Boys, boys," I soothed, "don't fight over me."

"We're not fighting over you," Wayne said.

"It's more a question of invading personal space, right, Wayne?" Peter said.

Wayne nodded. "Yeah, I guess so," he said uncertainly.

I glared at them. "You don't leave a girl any illusions, do you guys?"

I shouldn't really have expected them to fight. Wayne is a hunk, but no athlete. And he'd hate to have his face marred. But it was a letdown.

"What's personal space?" he asked.

"Well, it's like—have you ever heard of the territorial imperative?"

"Guys," I said. "This is very irritating."

"No." Wayne shook his head. "What's the territorial whatever?"

"*Guys!* I take back what I said. Fight over me."

I looked at Peter. He had a mischievous gleam in his eye. I looked at Wayne. He was frowning, suggesting an intellectual curiosity no one ever knew he had.

143

Peter was right. This was history-making.

"Listen," I said loudly. "Wayne, we have to stop seeing each other."

"We haven't even started!"

"Check. So your sorrow at losing me won't last too long."

"Aw, Joey."

"Don't whine, Wayne. It's unmanly."

April Abruzzo strolled by our table. "Hi, guys," she said. She tossed her honey-gold hair.

Wayne leaped up from the bench and nearly vaulted over the table. "Hi...April..." he breathed into her ear.

"'Bye, Wayne," Peter said. He shifted around and grinned at me. "Fast healer, isn't he?"

"Are you deliberately trying to annoy me?" I demanded.

"Yeah. How'm I doing so far?"

My head was spinning. Things were getting awfully confusing again. It was hard to keep track. I lost Wayne. Peter lost Dinah. I didn't want Wayne. Dinah didn't want Peter. Cockeyed Harry wanted me. I didn't want Cockeyed Harry commercials. But TV...?

And what did Peter want?

Fifteen

"I want to tell you something."

Peter got up from the floor and stretched. We were in my family room, and there was no one in the place except him and me. We'd worked two hours on Saturday's show, and the only non–show business we'd talked about was Cockeyed Harry's inspiration to make me his female spokesperson.

"Depending," Peter said, "on how you look on camera."

"How do I know how I'll look on camera?"

"Once he sees you cross your eyes, you're in. Don't think of it as doing commercials, think of it as doing TV. Lots of big stars started this way. Meantime you'll be making money."

I'll think of it. I'll give it a great deal of thought. It's probably an incredible opportunity. In fact, I ought to be going "Oooh! Oooh!" at the very idea of being on

TV, and I will—just as soon as I can think straight, and the last show is over, and I figure out what's going on in my love life. Or if I'm going to have one.

Now, as Peter paced the room, he seemed moody and preoccupied again.

"I'm not seeing Dinah anymore." His voice was very low.

I watched him prowl around the room. I craned my neck, following his route.

"You must be pretty upset," I said carefully.

"The only reason I let her on the program was because I had the—I mean, because I was attracted to her."

"I know exactly what you mean." *And I hate hearing you say it.*

But he was talking to me! He was telling me deep, important, meaningful things, revealing his true emotions. Talk about history-making! Even if I didn't like what he was telling me, this was a breakthrough. Who could tell what might break through next?

"So you would have let her on the show," I said calmly, "even if she sang like Godzilla?"

"Yeah. Maybe not to sing, but I'd have found something for her to do."

I can imagine.

I cleared my throat. I had to be careful here. Peter's ego was wounded, and if he was going to get over Dinah and come to me for love at last, I'd have to be very tactful as he admitted the sordid details of his love affair.

146

He stopped pacing and flopped on the couch. "I couldn't help it, Joey. I was—I was—"

"Crazed with lust?" I suggested. All right, so tact isn't my strong point.

He leaned his hands on his knees and gazed at me steadily. "I liked her. And yes, if you want the truth, when she was my lab partner I had the highest test tube breakage record in the history of the school."

Maybe baring your soul is overrated. Maybe I don't need to know so much about Peter's private feelings. Maybe we can communicate without being so painfully honest.

"I get the picture." I tried to keep the bitterness out of my voice. "She had you nibbling your beakers, you've been dreaming of her ever since, and when she asked—"

"No, it wasn't like that. After the first couple of weeks, when I saw it was hopeless, I gave up. It just got—uh—stirred up again when she asked if she could sing on the show.

"And she was very honest," he went on. "She told me right at the beginning that she was grateful to me, but she wasn't sure she felt anything else."

He shrugged his shoulders. "I figured it was a start. It was better than nothing. And you were acting so weird, like you hated me all of a sudden. And Dinah was being so nice to me."

"How nice?"

He hit me with those straight-on, honest eyes again. "Nice," he said evenly.

147

I closed my eyes and tried not to think what that might mean.

"And then you told me you liked me, and I couldn't believe it because you never acted like—I mean, you were always fooling around, you know, making jokes."

"But that's why you liked me!" I said. "You told me that. You wanted the laugh, clown, laugh bit. You even said I kissed funny."

"Joey, you were going out with Wayne Newberger. You were giving me blow-by-blow descriptions of your wrestling matches."

"That was last year! I was trying to make you jealous, you dimwit!" The hell with his delicate ego. "And I never let myself get pinned, did I?"

"How was I supposed to know that?" he asked. "You went out with other guys too, before that. And now you were starting up with him again—I mean, I thought you were trying to make it really clear that we were only friends."

Now I started prowling the room. I looked for something to kick. I wanted to pound my fists against the paneling. I wanted to scream in frustration. All these years, shot, because neither of us had the nerve, or the common sense, to express a perfectly natural emotion.

You blind fool. Can't you see what I'm trying to tell you? I wasn't sure who I was saying it to.

"I only went out with Wayne for a little while," I said. "You had plenty of time to say something."

Years.

"I was afraid you'd laugh at me."

"You weren't afraid Dinah would laugh?"

148

"Dinah doesn't have much of a sense of humor," he said. "And that Peter Zero bit—all these girls who never noticed me before started talking to me. It sort of built up my confidence. And now that I know how you feel—"

"What? Now that you know how I feel, what are you saying? That you don't have Dinah anymore, so you'll settle for me?"

"*I'm not settling,*" he said. "I'm saying what I wanted to say for a year."

"A year?" He's only loved me for a year? For some weird reason that made me feel a little better. At least I didn't have to regret wasting four years. Just one.

"I'm not saying I can forget Dinah overnight," he said.

"How long do you think it'll take?"

"I don't know. It just happened. Maybe it's mostly my ego that's hurt."

"So you want me to kiss it and make it better?" I guess I sounded sarcastic, but it was hard not to think that I was Peter's second choice.

He gave me a sheepish little grin. "Yeah. I'd like that."

"Do you know how much you hurt me?" I said quietly. "Not just—I mean, when you did your Peter Zero number. You were *mean.* You didn't care about my feelings. You didn't care what you did to me on the air. I have an ego too, you know."

"You don't just have an ego," he said. "You have an EGO."

I nodded.

"I'm sorry," he said unhappily. "I really am. It was so much pressure, and I felt like I was torn three different ways at once. I didn't mean to hurt you—I just didn't know how to deal with all of it. You were so—listen, you weren't too easy to handle, Joey. And I didn't understand all the reasons why."

"I know." I hesitated. "I'm very bad at sharing the spotlight. I don't know how I'm going to feel thinking that when you're with me you'll be wishing I was Dinah."

"Would it help if I told you that sometimes when I was with Dinah I wished she was you?"

I sank down on the nearest chair. "Really? Is that really true?" I started to shiver. I had to grip my hands together to keep them from shaking.

He nodded. "It's true."

His voice made me shiver even more.

"Oh, Peter."

He exhaled, like he'd been holding his breath for a long time. His whole body seemed to relax like a tight spring uncoiling. He leaned back on the couch and we looked at each other for a while. Just looked. Maybe so we'd always remember. Or maybe because we never looked hard enough before.

Now, I thought dizzily, now is the time to sing the Hallelujah Chorus. But I didn't want to sing. I wanted to stay right here, feeling Peter love me at last, knowing that he'd loved me before I knew it. Dinah was just a brief distraction for him, as unimportant as Wayne Newberger.

150

He hadn't recovered yet, he'd admitted that. But I was his first choice all along.

"What do we do now?" I asked timidly. I really wasn't sure. I knew what I wanted to do, but after not doing it for so long, how do you start?

He patted the sofa cushion next to him. "You could come over here and give my ego a serious, no-kidding-around kiss."

I didn't think my legs would carry me as far as the sofa. "No, you come here and kiss me. I kissed you first and you said I kiss funny. Let's see how you kiss."

I was so shy, so nervous. I'd never felt like this before. Not with anybody—never with Peter. But I'd never had my dream come true before, either.

"I'm no Wayne Newberger, you know." He stood up and approached me cautiously, like he was walking the last mile on death row. "It takes years of practice and hard work to get to be a Wayne Newberger."

"So what?" I murmured. "So for the first couple of years I'll carry you."

He took my hands in his and pulled me up from the chair.

"Peter, I'm nervous. Isn't that silly?"

He put his hands on my shoulders. "Yeah. Silly. Listen, you're not going to do anything funny, like cross your eyes at the last minute, are you?"

"I'll keep my eyes closed."

"Okay. Here goes." He sounded like he was preparing for a swan dive off the high board. He wrapped his arms around me and kissed me gently.

151

I'd imagined this so many times. My imagination never prepared me for the overpowering reality of my feelings.

He loosened his arms a little. "Was that okay?"

"Yes," I said shakily. "Definitely." I could hardly breathe.

"Oh, *Joey.*" He pulled me to him and held me tightly. "I wish I had the nerve to do this sooner."

"Me too." I put my arms around him and leaned my head against his chest.

I felt his heart beating. I could almost hear it.

And I knew that this minute had been worth all the hours I'd spent waiting for it.

Sixteen

"Hello out there in Radioland! I'm Peter Zero, coming to you on WRTP Radio 1301 for our third and last show. Joining me tonight is my co-host, Joey Merino...."

Co-host! He called me his co-host! What a beautiful gesture. I grew positively misty-eyed.

"...wish this were television, folks, so you could see the expression on Joey's face, just because I gave her a meaningless promotion on the last night of the show.

"She's speechless, and believe me, this is a girl who started talking at birth and hasn't shut up ever since."

Isn't he adorable? I thought. Isn't he the most adorable combination of Peter Zero and Peter Stillman?

And am I not pretty adorable myself? What with my irresistible mixture of razor-sharp wit and soft-hearted charm? Am I a sweetheart, or what?

I smiled lovingly at him. Maybe it had taken us awhile to get going, but years and years of utterly non-platonic friendship lay ahead of us.

Even as I sat dopey with love and rosy with optimisim, I thought about having lunch with Cockeyed Harry on Monday. About how he really seemed serious about this TV thing. If he did hire me, it could give me a fantastic opportunity to be discovered and rocket to fame and fortune.

Or it might happen tonight. At this very moment, somewhere out there in Radioland, a talent agent might be hunched over his radio waiting to hear Bronco Billy. But he'd hear my act first. He'd leap up from his chair and cry, "Eureka! A star is born!" And he'd race to his phone and dial Directory Assistance for WRTP's number.

"...but first a song filled with tender sentiment and meaningful lyrics. For all you romantics out there, let's listen to 'Giddyap, Giddyap, Giddyap, Whoa, My Pony Boy.'"

As Pony Boy trotted on, Peter turned to me with a look of concern. "Are you okay? You let me do the whole opening without interrupting me."

"The meaningless promotion overwhelmed me," I said. "Don't worry. With all those honchos listening for Bronco Billy, I'll be interrupting you all night."

He grinned. "Good. Because I need you." He leaned

over and gave me a quick kiss on the eyebrow. "I *really* need you. No joke."

"No joke," I said softly. I reached for his hands, and my fingers meshed with his.

I wasn't even tempted to cross my eyes.